LOVETAPS

LOVETAPS

C. L. Hoffman

iUniverse, Inc.
New York Lincoln Shanghai

Lovetaps

All Rights Reserved © 2003 by C. L. Hoffman

No part of this book may be reproduced or transmitted in any form or by any means, graphic, electronic, or mechanical, including photocopying, recording, taping, or by any information storage retrieval system, without the written permission of the publisher.

iUniverse, Inc.

For information address:
iUniverse, Inc.
2021 Pine Lake Road, Suite 100
Lincoln, NE 68512
www.iuniverse.com

ISBN: 0-595-29064-7

Printed in the United States of America

For Agnes,

*The perfect soul-mate
of former lives,
this life,
and lives to come…*

And for my parents, of course.

Contents

Foreword ix

Short Stories
The Song of Solomon Moscowitz 3
Brodsky in Paradise 25
A Trip to Town 40
The Seven Uncommon sons: A Fable 44
Brodsky in Transit 56
Lovetaps 70

Meditations
Home With Some Old Friends 97
The Trouble with Hebrew 100
A Note From School 103
He and She 106
Don't Worry Israel, Nothing is Forever 109
An Accidental Israeli 112
A Midwinter Night's Dream 116
Mr. Weissbord and Me 120

A Poem
1958 129

Foreword

The short stories and ruminations in this volume were written sporadically over a fifteen year period, 1987–2003. Only one of the short stories has been previously published, the rest appear here for the first time. "A Trip to Town" appeared in *Salaysayan* Magazine, published in the Philippines. The essays have all been published previously. "Home with Some Old Friends," "The Trouble with Hebrew," "A Note from School," and "He and She" all appeared in the *Jerusalem Post Magazine*. "Don't Worry Israel, Nothing is Forever" appeared in both the *Jerusalem Post Magazine* and *Esra* Magazine, which also published "An Accidental Israeli," and "A Midwinter Night's Dream." "Mr. Weissbord and Me" appeared, in a somewhat shortened form, in *City Lights* Magazine, published in Tel Aviv. The final poetry offering, "1958," appears in this book for the first time.

The short stories in this book are works of fiction. Any similarities between the characters or situations portrayed in the stories to actual persons or events are coincidental, unintended, and unfortunate.

C.L.H.

Short Stories

The Song of Solomon Moscowitz

The island of Boracay, nestled at the heart of the Philippine archipelago like a frail rare gem, shimmers brazenly and beautifully in a riot of blinding colors. Pearl of the Orient, one of God's most conspicuous successes. A brilliant magic trick of emerald green mountains tumbling down toward powdery white sand beaches, set against the crystal blue water of a calm inland sea. Gentle ocean currents caress the body; breezes drifting down from the verdant hillsides tease the senses with flirtatious hints of sweet jasmine and lush red bougainvillea.

A particularly glorious dawn broke over this South Sea Eden one April day, painting a rich tableau: Dappled morning sunlight dancing on the leaves of postcard-pretty coconut palm trees. Lush throngs of palms—growing along the dazzling white beach as far as the eye could see—arching lazily over scores of small, gaudily painted outrigger canoes lining the shore and bobbing gently in the shallow water. The almost syrup-like ocean sparkling azure blue, its calm surf whispering to the early morning sun. Multitudes of lavishly plumed bantam roosters joyously proclaiming the start of another exquisite day. And, still sluggish and nasally congested from sleep, Mr. Solomon Hersch Moscowitz—late of Long Island, N.Y. and now unleashed upon an unsuspecting world—yawning at the window of his little bamboo and thatch cottage set a few feet back from the beach, squinting into the morning sunlight, and fumbling open the small blue velvet bag containing his *yarmulke*, prayer shawl, and phylacteries.

"Yeah, well…first things first," Solomon mumbled drowsily, doing his best to ignore the vivid explosion of tropical colors and festive noises outside his open window—the sights and sounds of this, his first morning on Boracay, to which he had arrived, haggard but hopeful, on a crowded tourist ferry the previous afternoon. With a loud guttural yawn, he began with the *yarmulke*, slapping it onto the back of his head. Reminding himself in the process—once again—that his short red hair was beginning to thin noticeably, making him look a lot older than his 35 years.

Next came the black and white linen prayer shawl, which Moscowitz unfurled, kissed, intoned the appropriate prayer over, then tossed back over his narrow shoulders like a matador twirling a cape. Forcefully shaking off the last vestiges of sleep, Moscowitz now focused on the phylacteries, carefully unraveling the black leather straps.

As he had done countless times in the past, every morning since turning thirteen, Solomon softly murmured the opening benediction as he fitted the black leather box of the arm piece around the biceps of his skinny left arm.

"*Boruch atoh Adonoy, Elohenu Melech ha-Olom…*"

Two almost naked white tourists—a man and a woman, Germans probably, maybe French—strolled languidly by Moscowitz's cottage as Solomon continued romancing his arm phylactery. Seven times around the forearm, twice around the palm. His eyes took on a will of their own as they hungrily followed the large pallid woman's ample behind. Solomon quickly reasserted control, jerking his washed-out hazel eyes back with a snap toward the head piece of his phylacteries.

He gently kissed the head piece and placed it on his head, carefully positioning the black leather box at the beginning of his hairline—also starting to recede.

"*…Asher kidishonu beMitzvo-sov VeTzivonu…*" Solomon intoned, already rocking back and forth. "*…l' Haneach Tefillin…*"

The sharp odor of sizzling bacon and pungent pork sausages came wafting into his window from a small restaurant a few yards away as Moscowitz completed the final stage of winding the arm piece—three times around the middle finger, twice across the palm. Solomon sniffed the air and sneezed at the sacrilege.

A huge sunburned blond-haired man—middle aged and unmistakably Australian—stomped past the cottage, his arm around a hard faced Filipino girl who just barely came up to his waist. The girl looked to be around 16 or 17, going on 40. The Australian, despite the early hour, had his other hand wrapped tightly around a bottle of San Miguel beer. Standing at his window arrayed in full ceremonial regalia, facing toward what he guessed, roughly, was the general direction of Jerusalem, Moscowitz continued his prayers. As the couple loudly negotiated with an eager young hustler over the fee for a boat trip around the island, Solomon redoubled his concentration, rocking back and forth with increased fervor.

Solomon Moscowitz—self-styled urbane Citizen of the World and suave *bon vivant*—long ago stopped trying to explain to himself why he still bothered to do this every morning. God knew, he was no longer terribly religious. To tell the truth, he really couldn't say with any conviction that he even believed in God anymore. (It went without saying that no self-respecting God in his right mind could believe in Solomon Moscowitz.) For a while he had tried to rationalize the ritual, telling himself (along with incredulous friends and annoyed roommates awakened at ungodly hours of the morning) that it was "a form of meditation," that it "focused the mind," and "sharpened the senses." Solomon no longer wasted breath or strained credence with these excuses. He simply continued to schlepp out of bed and say his prayers at the crack of every dawn, long after sloughing off almost every other part of his religious observance, like a bird molting its feathers.

As Moscowitz neared the completion of his morning prayers, the island of Boracay was busily springing to life. Virtually all of the island's native inhabitants—rural Filipinos simultaneously thrilled and bewildered at Boracay's transformation from remote island to tourist Mecca—were now up, around, and going about their business. Or, more accurately, business*es*: serving food to tourists, providing them accommodations, taking them on boat rides, renting them wind-surfing rigs, fishing gear, and scuba-diving equipment. Chauffeuring them around the island on the backs of battered motorcycles. Attempting to sell them everything from floppy straw hats to suntan oil, tie-dyed T-shirts to lacquered tortoise shells, and even anatomically correct little wooden men in barrels—complete with leering grins and retractable penises.

And the tourists themselves, or at least the morning shift, were also now out in force—a "colorful" array of upscale travelers, downscale backpackers, noisy newlyweds, dour old couples, eternal hippies, social desperadoes, sun worshippers, sex trippers, and other specimens from virtually every country in the world.

Moscowitz completed his prayers and was about to begin the laborious process of removing and refolding his prayer shawl and phylacteries, when he happened to glance at the open door of his cottage. There at the doorway were maybe eight or ten Filipino children, the oldest barely nine years old, who had evidently been watching Solomon at his morning devotions. Still fully bedecked in his ritual equipage of white satin scull-cap, billowing black and white prayer shawl with shimmering fringe tassels, and little black leather boxes lodged at arm and forehead, Solomon studied the kids. And the kids (you can rest assured) studied Solomon, staring up at him in slack-jawed, wide-eyed wonder. For fully two minutes they all stood thus, transfixed in the moment and having a wonderful time.

After a quick breakfast of mango juice, toast, coffee, and a large wedge of soft ripe papaya, Moscowitz was ready to storm the beach. Though barely eight a.m., the tropical sun was already high and hot. Solomon marched out onto the warm white sand—a most improbable *Beau Geste,* arrayed in an impossibly huge straw hat purchased the day before from an old woman trolling the beach with over twenty of these monstrosities perched on her head. He was also equipped with a straw mat—rolled up and carried under his arm—and a large shoulder bag containing, among other odds-and-ends, travelers' cheques, passport, camera, several rolls of film, Pepto Bismol, a couple of unapologetically trashy paperbacks, a large aerosol spray can of OFF! mosquito repellent, a bottle of Tylenol, three bottles of Coppertone sun screen lotion (heavy duty, for extra protection), multiple bottles of prescription nasal spray, some Alka-Seltzer, more Pepto Bismol, a full role of toilet paper, some loose change in several currencies, and a half a roll of Certs. Not to mention some two dozen condoms, on 24 hour stand-by status since their purchase in New York several weeks ago, and now laying quietly, hopefully in their little foil packs deep at the bottom of the bag.

Moscowitz staked out a place in the sand, about ten yards away from a uniformly pink and plump German-speaking family of five on one side, and a good-natured gaggle of middle-aged Chinese matrons on the other, probably down from Taiwan. He pulled off his T-shirt, self-consciously sucking in his belly and flexing his muscles for the benefit of anyone passing by who might take the trouble to look. He needn't have bothered. No one was looking, and Solomon had nothing much really to "flex."

At five feet, eleven inches, and weighing in at barely 120 lbs., Solomon's body was attracting no attention, aside from that indiscriminately bestowed to one and all from the wandering vendors of straw hats, mats, T-shirts and other bric-a-brac. Moscowitz presented an eminently forgettable portrait: narrow shoulders, protruding ribs, skinny legs with knobby knees. Pallid skin, a long bony face crowned with thinning hair. Sad dreamy eyes sandwiched between a high narrow forehead and a long nose curving downward toward a wide mouth with thin pale lips.

Solomon began to apply a hefty coating of Coppertone to his arms and shoulders, already lobster-red from yesterday afternoon. He thought fleetingly of ozone holes and ultra-violet rays. He unrolled his wicker mat and sat down, enjoying the rich blue color of the ocean in front of him. Solomon unzipped his shoulder bag and started rummaging around for some nasal spray, remembering suddenly an old joke from his college roommate. After lying awake for most of a night listening to Solomon sneeze and wheeze—emblems of chronic allergy—this clever young wag had speculated that sinus congestion was responsible for at least 50% of Moscowitz's body weight.

Probing at the bottom of the bag, Solomon's hand pounced upon its prey. Unscrewing the cap of the nasal spray and inserting nozzle **A** into nostril **B**, Moscowitz glanced sideways in time to see three young women walking in his general direction. Filipino, all in their early twenties. Manila girls, of the sort produced by well-heeled families. College types, dressed, from top down, in baseball caps, dark green Ray-Ban sunglasses with bright red cords attached, tight halter tops exposing sleek brown arms and shoulders, very short striped walking shorts girded with black rayon money belts, shapely muscled legs ending in white ankle-socks and pricey black running shoes. Solomon's bottle of nasal spray fell from his limp hand into the sand, never to be seen again. He sat and stared as the girls approached.

The three young women strolled by Moscowitz as though he were vapor. One inadvertently kicked a bit of sand at him as she walked by. Solomon rose quickly from his mat and plunged into the warm blue water—to get out of the hot sun, and to hide a very large, very painful erection.

Lunch time found Moscowitz alone and spread out at a table on the beach. He had commandeered the table—and all six chairs—at an outdoor cafe huddled in the shadows of two arching palm trees, desperately seeking surfeit from the midday sun. Solomon attempted to signal the place's sole waitress, a cute but frazzled looking local girl who shuffled slowly around in her beat-up plastic sandals, without ever seeming to lift her feet from the sand. As she slouched by Solomon's table, the girl raised a flaccid hand and muttered, "for a while, sir," the smile on her face—almost a smirk—reflecting some deep inner joke known only to her.

Solomon shrugged and swung his shoulder bag up onto the table, from which he extracted a small loose-leaf notebook and a Bic pen. He figured he'd start a long-postponed letter to his brother while settling back to wait for the waitress. His brother David ("David and Solomon." Their parents had had a vague, if undeveloped sense of humor), older than Solomon by nine years, married, three children. And a highly successful (read: **prosperous**) proctologist. "*Ungestupped with money!*" was the expression used with unabashed admiration by their late father Harry to describe the attainments of his elder and favorite son.

Comfortably, if grimly ensconced in the suburban splendor of Hempstead, L.I. with his perennially tanned, figure salon-taut wife and their three overwrought, overweight teenage daughters, David Moscowitz was "not amused" by his younger brother Solomon. Solomon the Seeker. Solomon the Not-so-Wise, Solomon the Space Cadet. Solomon the *Schlemiel.* Solomon—in David's opinion since childhood—the whining pain in the ass. Solomon the short-distance runner who had, in fairly orderly succession, dropped out of medical school, out of law school, out of graduate school, and out of their father's wholesale furniture business—a make-work job dreamed up by David and their father as a last-ditch effort to find something for Solomon to do. Not to mention dropping out of much of his religious observance, out of the country, and now—apparently—out of reality.

"And I guess out of the family," Solomon reflected sadly as he scratched at a blank page with his Bic to get the pen to write. For truth to tell, his brother David was now all Solomon had left in the way of family following the abrupt demise of their father several months ago. Harry Moscowitz, aged 72, had keeled over and dropped dead onto the floor of "Moscowitz's Discount Furniture Emporium," in the middle of a particularly impassioned argument over the phone with one of his accountants. The boys' mother, the soft spoken and almost invisible Bea Moscowitz, had died during Solomon's sophomore year in college at N.Y.U. Bea departed the world at precisely the time she might have had some salutary, moderating effect on each of her two sons. Who knows?—she may have been able to get David the Driven to calm down and live a little, while giving her "less motivated" younger son Solomon the swift kick in the ass he so badly needed. Instead she succumbed to cancer after a long hard year, leaving her sons to Harry. Harry, whose very existence had somehow served to reinforce the differences in his sons' personalities, and whose dramatic departure seven months ago had weakened, if not severed, the last link Solomon had with his brother, family and home.

"*Excuse me*, is someone sitting here?"

Startled, Moscowitz looked up from his notebook into the eyes of a young Asian woman—Filipino, almost certainly—bending slightly toward him with a slight, tentative smile.

"Huh?" was Solomon's clever reply.

"I'm sorry to disturb you," the young woman soldiered on, "but all of the other tables are full. *Is* anyone else sitting here?"

Moscowitz looked around and saw that the tables had indeed filled while he'd been daydreaming. A garishly colorful parade of humanity was streaming by the cafe, clad in everything from batik sarongs to scuba-diving suits.

"Ah...no. *No*, no one, Nobody's sitting here. I'm alone," sputtered Solomon, gesturing nervously toward the empty chairs.

"Then may I sit here and take my lunch?" the girl asked, her smile spreading into something truly radiant.

Solomon was already violently jerking his head up and down, which the girl fortunately interpreted as a sign of assent. Tossing an artsy looking native shoulder basket onto one of the empty chairs, she sat down opposite Moscowitz and said, "Thanks. I really like the food here, especially the mango and pineapple milkshakes. Even though they are bad for my figure." She patted an absolutely flat stomach and laughed softly, musically.

Moscowitz glanced reflexively at the young woman's "figure" and found it virtually flawless. Maybe 5' 4", small-boned, perfectly proportioned. A slender woman, delicate looking. Solomon almost had to reach up and force his head downwards by hand in order to avoid staring.

Perhaps prompted by the arrival of the young woman, the waitress—yawning and smirking—finally flounced by their table and slid two large plastic-covered menus between them. As the young woman studied her menu, Moscowitz peeked over the top of his, continuing his study of the new arrival.

Thick, almost coarse black hair, shoulder length and luxuriant, adorned with two bright red hair clips. Large almond-shaped eyes, a short broad nose, and full generous lips. A bit heavy on the make-up, thought Solomon; eyebrows a little too carefully tweezed. She was wearing a tight green halter-top whose bottom did not quite meet the top of her tight jeans, and which displayed bare, rich-brown shoulders and arms. To say nothing of small, but high firm breasts. The girl, Solomon decided, was more sexy than "pretty," yet somehow exuding a vague a sense of vulnerability, of fragility. Moscowitz sat and gaped.

There was one other thing that Moscowitz noticed. Something indefinable, yet very real. Solomon guessed that this young woman did not move in the same social world as the upscale yuppie wannabies he had seen strolling the beach all day. Despite the make-up and hip fashionable clothes, something about this girl—a darker complexion, a certain overall *look*—said "earthy," "rural," "provincial."

As she perused the menu, the young woman absently moistened her very red lips with her tongue. Moscowitz swallowed hard and hurled his eyes onto his menu. Nervously scanning the document, Solomon decided it could aptly be titled *"101 Ways to Cook Swine."* While Solomon continued to observe Jewish holidays and say his morning prayers with unstinting regularity, he no longer felt strictly bound by Jewish dietary laws. He followed the broad outlines but blinked at the fine points. Needless to say, it was virtually impossible to travel the world and expect to find things like two separate sets of dishes and silverware for meat and dairy wherever he happened to stop. Solomon relaxed and went with the flow, to the point of developing a particular, if guilt-ridden fondness for shrimp and lobster.

Moscowitz still had a problem with pork, though. No matter what else he'd been able to rationalize and then eat, pork was still the "Final Frontier." Solomon occasionally wondered why, and eventually decided it had something to do with "racial memory." Perhaps, he figured, for over three millennia of Jewish history, the pig had vividly embodied all that was alien, all that was *trayf* and, perhaps aesthetically, all that was wrong with gentile cuisine. Whatever, the very thought of biting into any one of the choices offered on this menu made something deep inside Solomon want to hurry down into a cellar and hide until the Cossacks rode away from the *shtetl*.

"You look a little confused. Can I help?"

Moscowitz glanced up quickly to find the young woman staring at him, with a smile that could have tamed those Cossacks and warmed the Russian steppes. The girl made a gesture with her lips—pursed them and used them to point to the menu in Solomon's hand.

"Filipino food. *Very* delicious. Would you like me to help you choose something? There are *many* good things," she offered hospitably.

Moscowitz immediately fell in love with the young woman's accent. Sort of Hispanic, vaguely like Mexican, but with an Oriental lilt he had never quite heard before. Her voice was soft and soothingly cool.

The waitress returned, God only knew what was holding her upright. Solomon gave up on finding something he could eat and handed her back his menu.

"I guess I'll just have a cup of coffee," he droned mournfully, shrugging his narrow shoulders.

With a quick glance at Solomon, the young woman gave her menu to the waitress, a rapid exchange of Tagalog passing between them. The waitress took the menus and ambled off toward the kitchen, moving noticeably faster than usual.

Moscowitz shrugged again and murmured apologetically, "I had a really big breakfast. I guess I'm not terribly hungry." He smiled at her nervously, trying to think of something to say.

"So, how do you like Boracay?" was the best he could do.

The girl's smile faded for an instant. She said, "Oh, I like it very much. This is my third time here." Her face took on a distracted, and distinctly serious look.

Wondering what the hell he'd said wrong, Solomon gushed, "My first time. And I'm really glad I came…never saw a prettier beach."

The young woman sat back in her chair and studied Moscowitz for a long moment. Thoughtfully and, for an instant, pensively—as though she was trying to make up her mind about something.

"Well, if we are going to be sharing a table, I think maybe we should introduce ourselves," she said finally, her broad smile returning. "My name is Chris." The small, delicate hand she held out toward Solomon was ornamented with a small gold bracelet, gold rings on two fingers, and bright red nail polish. Solomon gently grasped her outstretched hand. The palm and fingers were an instant surprise—the skin unexpectedly hard and rough.

"Chris?" repeated Solomon, almost blanching at the name.

"Yes sir," she replied. "Actually, my full name is Maria…Christina…Elena…Dominguez." She pronounced the names separately, accentuating each with a graceful movement of her other hand. "Please just call me Chris, okay?"

"No problem," said Solomon smiling, letting go of her hand. He was liking this woman's accent more and more. "I'm Solomon Moscowitz."

"What-what???" she blurted, jerking forward in her chair.

"*Solomon*, like in the Bible," he said patiently, "and *Moscowitz*, like in…" he trailed off, doubtfully.

"Like in Moscow, of course!" Chris piped in brightly. "Are you from, what is it…Russia?"

"No, I'm American," Solomon began, to the young woman's obvious confusion. But before he could launch into what would undoubtedly have been a most illuminating dissertation on the subject of Eastern European Jewish surnames, the waitress sailed over to their table, bearing a heavy cargo. She placed before Chris a steaming plate of white rice topped with some sort of chopped meat and vegetables.

"This is called *menudo*—very good," Chris said to Solomon helpfully.

Moscowitz got a cup of hot water, about two thirds full, with a small jar of Nescafe Classic, a bowl of sugar, and a tiny glass pitcher of what appeared to be evaporated milk. As Solomon prepared to create a cup of coffee from these diverse elements, he glanced up and saw that the waitress was not yet finished disgorging her load. She thumped down a plate containing the largest pancake Moscowitz had ever seen, with a cute little container of syrup.

"Hey wait a minute, I didn't order this," said Solomon nervously as the waitress set down his silverware and a folded paper napkin.

"Banana and pineapple pancake," Chris explained as she poured syrup rather liberally onto Solomon's plate. "*I* ordered it for you—my treat."

Embarrassed, Solomon began to protest. Chris simply smiled her radiant smile and said, "Eat."

As the waitress freshened her smirk and walked away—faster than a speeding bullet, Moscowitz shoveled a syrup-heavy piece of pancake into his mouth. It was, Solomon quickly realized, the most delicious pancake he had ever had in his whole life.

Nighttime on Boracay is also a work of art. Delightfully cool, the heat of the day already fading into tired, happy memory. Gentle fragrant breezes. Quiet muted colors. The calm moonlit sea shimmering beneath a velvet, starlit sky. Palm trees swaying high above, softly whispering their nighttime secrets.

All is festive back a bit from the beach in the hours of early evening. Raucous and glaringly colorful, almost like a carnival. Tourists from almost every place on earth promenade up and down the little footpath, gaudily dressed up in what each of their disparate cultures considers appropriate for 'an evening on a tropical isle.' Hawaiian shirts, Panama hats, white pants, cotton dresses, sarongs and short-shorts define their wearers as they parade by brightly lit shops, quiet candle-lit restaurants, and cozy little bars. The restaurants, of course, proudly offer the island's rich bounty of fabulous fresh seafood; and the cozy little bars coyly offer picturesque, elaborately named cocktails—"South Sea Pirate," "Zombie," "Blue Lagoon," etc.—each served in a hollowed-out pineapple shell and festooned with the inevitable paper umbrella.

At a small table-for-two in a crowded beachside restaurant, Solomon Moscowitz sat expectantly, eagerly scanning the crowds strolling by. Craning his long sunburnt neck, Solomon was visibly excited, and happier than he'd been in many, many months.

"No sense denying it," thought Solomon to himself, "I'm in love."

A heady heart-thumping exuberance, mixed with confusion, took hold of Moscowitz as he tried to make some sense of the day. His impromptu lunch with this intoxicating young lady Chris had somehow expanded to fill most of the afternoon. *Maria Christina Elena Dominguez*—he had loved the way her accent seemed to dance across her name and had asked her to repeat it five or six times through the meal. She gladly obliged, with her magnificent smile and her soft musical laughter.

Solomon could not get over how long they had sat and talked. He had been almost totally oblivious to the passing scene. To say nothing of the passing time. Chris, however, had occasionally peered over his shoulder at one or another passing tourist, as though she'd recognized him from somewhere. Moscowitz barely noticed, mesmerized by her smile, her voice.

For Solomon, Chris had been like a drug, or more accurately, like falling off the wagon after a long period of abstinence and taking that first mind-blasting, blood-boiling drink. It had been well over a year since his last relationship, and that one had been no great shakes. Judy "Take-No-Prisoners" Blumberg had been a year older than Moscowitz when the two of them had met through mutual friends. She had seemed at least fifteen years older to Solomon by the time they had finally decided to disengage and cast their respective nets back into the water.

After a couple of false nibbles, Judy had managed to hook, reel-in and land a very promising, up-and-coming tax lawyer and junior partner at a prestigious Wall Street law firm. A man worthy of her intelligence, maturity and, thought Solomon with more than a trace of bitterness, her mindless ambition. Solomon simply drifted after the engagement was over, through endless dead days at his father's discount furniture warehouse, through his father's theatrical death and burial, through the tense period of mourning—marked by endless arguments about anything and everything with his brother David. And through a getaway-from-it-all vacation to Hawaii, the South Pacific, and points beyond. The first real vacation he had ever taken. Moscowitz had withdrawn his meager savings and had chosen the general island-bound direction to get as far away from home as the curvature of the earth would allow.

Drifting.

Until today.

Conversation with Chris had flowed easily; Solomon quickly realized he'd been desperate for it. He recited to her his autobiography, his 35-year saga of boredom and aimlessness, of being a celebrated wise guy and all-around *nudzh*. Chris had seemed genuinely interested, and had politely interrupted with some remarkably insightful questions.

Chris was articulate in an unadorned, straightforward way. She was born and raised, he told him, on an island called Samar, far to the south and east. She had come from a poor family, and had no education beyond her ramshackle, small-town high school. Like so many poor girls from her part of the country, she had tearfully left home and boarded a rickety inter-island ferry at the age of eighteen, to live with a distant relative in Manila, and to work and support her family back home. Chris was now 24, and had been working in Manila "at different jobs" for six years, faithfully sending money home to her vast extended family.

They sat and talked—"*shmoozed*," according to Moscowitz—until well after 4:00 in the afternoon. Drinking each other in. As their table became blanketed in spreading shadow, Chris stood, stretched, and to Solomon's enraptured delight, softly suggested they meet somewhere later for dinner.

Chris smiled that irresistible smile, gave Solomon her hand for a brief instant and then glided off, tossing her rattan bag over her shoulder. Solomon sat and stared as this small lithe girl receded into the passing crowd; his heart pounding, his sinuses aching. Unable to believe his pure dumb luck.

Still unable to believe it as he sat now, at precisely 10 minutes after 7:00, nervously waiting for Chris to re-emerge from the crowd and join him for dinner. Moscowitz glanced at his watch, for perhaps the twentieth time in the last two minutes, and cringed.

"Oh God, she probably wised up and changed her mind," Solomon moaned inwardly.

Chris had seemed suddenly evasive when Solomon had asked where she was staying, offering to come by for her at dinner time. The question had formed the only dark cloud over their golden afternoon together, however brief and insignificant. Moscowitz decided not to push and had let the matter drop. They simply agreed to meet, at 7:00 sharp, at a large torch-lit restaurant on the beach. A particularly successful venture, rumored to be owned by a beer-besotted old German of questionable background, the place drew tourists like flies to fire with a lavish all-you-can-eat buffet for the price of 100 Philippine pesos—a little less than $4.00.

Now inching toward 7:20, the place was already jumping. The full tables were illuminated by brightly colored Chinese lanterns; the immense, groaning buffet table lit by huge torches lashed to nearby palm trees. Solomon sat alone at a table, nursing a now lukewarm bottle of Sprite, almost beside himself with impatience. And panic. Afraid she would not come. Desperately afraid he'd never set eyes on her again.

As he sat savoring his self pity like fine wine, Moscowitz felt a tap on his shoulder. He jerked around and there she was, laughing softly and covering her smile with her hand.

Chris beamed and said, "*Shalom aleichem* Solomon...Did I say it right?"

Moscowitz fell in love with her all over again. "Spoken like a pro," he replied, flooded with happiness and relief. He stood up and held out a chair for her. "You're late," he blurted before he could stop himself.

Chris checked her watch as she sat down, pursed her lips in a look of mock contrition. "I came on time, Solomon. We call it 'Philippine Time.'" she said. Laughing that laugh.

A waiter, clad in what appeared to be the restaurant's staff uniform of loud Hawaiian shirt, faded cut-offs and fringy straw hat, materialized from nowhere to take their orders for drinks. Moscowitz—no drinker—asked for another Sprite. Chris, to Solomon's unspoken but obvious surprise, ordered herself a pitcher of beer. She caught the look on Solomon's face, smiled nervously, and gestured toward the buffet table.

"Let's get our dinner now, okay?" She rose and headed toward the torch light. Solomon followed her, feeling a vague unease.

However, Moscowitz's feelings, along with who knows how many brain cells, were quickly and violently flushed from his mind as he got close enough to the buffet table to see what was lying on it. Set down ceremoniously as the centerpiece of the table and glistening with greasy exuberance, was an entire roast pig—hideously intact from snout to tail. Moscowitz winced at this obscenity with Jungian horror.

"We call this *'lechon baboy'*—roast pig," Chris said as she handed a plate to Solomon and got one for herself. "What would you call it in your, ah...Jewish language?"

"*Trayf*," replied Solomon, desperately scanning the long table for other food.

As Chris lustily yanked pieces of tender white flesh and crisp brown skin from the recumbent pig, Moscowitz wandered around the table and helped himself to some delicious looking roast chicken, huge fried shrimp, spoonfuls of three different vegetable side dishes, along with wedges of papaya and very ripe, red watermelon. Solomon's Sprite and Chris' pitcher of San Miguel Beer were waiting at their table upon their return.

As they settled down to eat and talk—the initial hectic moments of meeting and food gathering now past—Solomon took a moment to check out his lovely companion. 'Lovely,' did not do her justice. Chris looked absolutely smashing in a low-cut red blouse and tight white crepe pants. A gold necklace sparkled against her flawless honey-brown skin; her thick black hair lustrous and adorned with red and gold clips. He realized he'd been wrong in his initial judgment; this girl was every bit as "pretty" as she was "sexy," and she was very, *very* sexy.

Chris beamed at him and said, "You look very…what is the word?…*'suave!'* Yes, suave…and very handsome. My *handsome* King Solomon!"

Moscowitz stared dumbly at Chris, still unable to believe his sheer, idiot luck. He finally summoned the presence of mind to say, "You look…you're the most beautiful woman I've ever laid eyes on."

Chris pondered this idiom for just an instant, unveiled her radiant smile and laughed. Crinkling her nose she said, "No, no…I'm really very ugly. Everyone in my family always said so, and they were right. I think maybe you need to get glasses, okay?" The smile. More laughter. Moscowitz could feel whatever was left of his defenses melting like ice in the sun.

Dinner moved along at a slow, measured pace. Moscowitz went back for seconds of everything, his eyes carefully avoiding the pig. Chris had more fruit and briefly toyed with the idea of ordering one more short mug of beer. "I want, but I'm embarrassed to order," she laughed.

Solomon paid the check—ridiculously cheap for what they'd just had—and off they went, locked in tight embrace. They strolled idly for a while, past brightly lit shops and food stalls. Barbecue skewers covered end-to-end with pieces of marinated pork or chicken lay sizzling on charcoal braziers, fanned by hot and very bored looking women and girls. Loud rock music thundered out of some of the shops; a few of the bars featured music videos on fancy VCRs and big-screen TVs.

Solomon and Chris breezed along until they came to something that seemed to be passing as a disco—loud music, revolving bright lights, dancing couples blurred and indistinct in the smoky haze. They peered into the entrance uncertainly.

Chris asked, "Do you want to go in?"

"I'm not really much of a dancer," demurred Moscowitz, true to form.

Chris brushed her hand across his back, his blue knit jersey now damp in the night heat. "Okay, then. I think I got a better idea," she murmured, leading Solomon away.

She led them down onto the beach, close to the water's edge. The sand was moist and cool. Tiny waves rolled softly ashore as the empty boats bobbed gently on the still water. Solomon and Chris found a place on the sand, secluded and enveloped in dark shadow.

In less than an instant, they were in each other's arms.

"Wow!" thought Solomon as he and Chris silently rejoined the promenading throngs a couple of hours later. He had just made love—*love!*—with the most exquisite woman he had ever seen—a woman he was definitely in love with, and one who clearly appeared to be in love with him. A woman, he was certain, who had made love with him because she liked him, and had genuinely wanted to.

Not like his ex-fiancée, he recalled sourly, who had gone to bed with him after something like their tenth date. Grudgingly—almost as though she were doing him a favor. He strongly suspected at the time that she had done this to prove some kind of point to her mother.

This, on the other hand, was love. Straightforward, guileless love. Moscowitz was enraptured, almost crazed.

They wandered along past shops and cafes, absorbed in companionable silence. Chris proposed stopping for a while in a little snack bar for coffee. Their eyes felt the glare of the shop's bright lights. Solomon noticed that Chris looked pensive again, preoccupied.

When they had given their orders, Chris placed her hand on Moscowitz's wrist and said gently, "King Solomon my love, I will be leaving here tomorrow. I'll go back to Manila."

As Moscowitz tried to absorb the shock she continued, "I came here with…somebody, a companion." Before he could speak she held up her hand and said, "That person left here yesterday, but I still have my return air ticket, and I must use it."

"No problem," Solomon said tensely, "we can just change the date of your flight."

"No, Solomon…I can't stay longer. I am expected back at work."

Moscowitz had a fleeting thought that if he could survive this moment without dropping dead, he could probably survive anything—up to and including global thermonuclear holocaust. Chris studied the look on his face and said, "Okay…look, no problem, huh? You're going to Manila after you finish here, right? Everyone does. So okay, I'll give you my address."

She took a bright pink plastic hair brush out of her purse and began to fish around for a pen. Writing her address on a paper napkin, she said "This is where I live. You go there when you get to Manila. I will be waiting for you."

Moscowitz grabbed the napkin with a shaking hand. As he studied the address, Chris leaned forward, held his wrist tighter and said, "Come in the daytime…okay, Solomon. Late morning is best."

Solomon started to speak but Chris cut him off, sharply. She let go of his wrist, looked at him penetratingly and said again, "Come there in the daytime. Do not come at night, okay?"

Solomon awakened the following morning with the cacophony of the island's roosters. Thoughts of Chris—her face, her voice, the smell of her hair—flooded his mind before he had even opened his eyes. God help him, he was standing at his window a moment later in his *yarmulke*, prayer shawl and phylacteries, without any conscious memory of having put them on. He may well have been worshipping Chris as he ploughed through his morning prayers.

Moscowitz knew better than to try to meet her and see her off. Chris had been adamant in making him promise to 'just let her go,' and to save their next meeting for Manila.

Poor Solomon, his plane ticket was for three days hence. And the owner of his cottage—accustomed to the flighty ways of foreign tourists—had made him pay for his entire stay in advance.

"How the hell am I going to get through the next three days," Solomon moaned aloud as he put away his prayer shawl and phylacteries.

He did his best. After languidly picking at his breakfast of scrambled eggs and toast, Moscowitz plunged into the crystal blue water for which Boracay is famous. No dice: the vivid image of Maria Christina Elena Dominguez came bounding back to him every time he closed his eyes underwater.

He considered a lesson in scuba diving. When he went to sign up however, the diving instructor—a tall stocky New Zealander with windblown hair and sunburnt face—took one look at Moscowitz and advised him, wisely, to go take a nice relaxing boat ride instead.

Solomon thought next of wind surfing, quickly came to his senses, and instead joined a small excursion group on a boat tour around the island. Sitting amidst a loud squawking family of hard-edged Koreans, an angry-looking Belgian couple, two obviously gay Norwegians, and a half-dead old German accompanied by his barely pubescent Filipino girlfriend, Solomon rocketed toward a quick decision.

Before the boat had even stopped moving at the end of the tour, Moscowitz had jumped off the gunwale and was charging up the beach, like something out of old newsreel footage of U.S. Marines landing at Iwo Jima. As swift as a gazelle, Solomon sprinted up to the booking office and changed his flight to Manila for early the following morning. Enough *naarishkeit*. And to hell with the advance payments on the cottage.

"And to hell with this *verkuckte* airline," Solomon mumbled to himself angrily, sitting, waiting, and gnashing his teeth at the small provincial airport the following day. And he had continued to sit and wait, first sullenly and then half out of his mind, through a lengthening delay of what turned out to be eight hours. Eight hours of listening to almost unintelligible loudspeaker announcements to the flight's passengers, apologizing for everything from engine trouble to "acts of God." Moscowitz found it hard to blame God for his antipathy toward this airline.

It was thus around 7:00 in the evening that Solomon's originally scheduled late-morning "brunch flight," having spent almost the entire day drawn into a flightless cocoon, had finally spread its wings and metamorphosed into its final form as a "dinner time trip." Moscowitz joined the crazed herd of fellow passengers elbowing their way aboard.

Landing in Manila about an hour later, Solomon had only one thing on his mind: making his way to Chris without another moment's delay. He waited for his bulky blue travel bag almost in a trance, and had barely any memory of jumping into a taxi and handing the driver the little paper napkin with Chris' address.

As the taxi hacked its way through the lush, almost impenetrable jungle of Manila's street traffic, Moscowitz nervously checked his watch and noted it was now almost 9:00 p.m. As the taxi inched slowly forward, Solomon's mind was working at 120 miles per hour. He would show up at Chris's place and be treated to an ecstatic reunion. He imagined that, once things settled down, he would either be invited to stay there with her—Chris would insist—or be lodged at a relative's house nearby. Or if she were still living with an aunt, a gaggle of small cousins and whatnot, maybe he and Chris would simply slip quietly away and check into an inexpensive but reasonably nice hotel. Solomon was so excited he could barely sit still—due in part to the fact that he'd been too preoccupied on the airplane to remember to visit a men's room.

Of course he remembered that Chris had asked him not to show up at night. But Moscowitz figured it was not a problem. If all of her relatives were home for the night, he and Chris could go out. Or if Chris was out with friends for the evening, he would simply wait around until she got home. No big deal.

Solomon was almost oblivious to his surroundings as the taxi came to a stop. The driver turned and handed back the paper napkin with Chris' address, pointed silently toward a nearby building, and took Moscowitz's fare and tip. Solomon hurried into the building, saw nothing but a narrow flight of wooden stairs heading upwards, and went bounding up the stairs two at a time.

He reached the top and found himself in a large cavernous room, with unpainted wooden walls, laundry hanging everywhere, and lots of beds. A faint, old smell of fried fish. To Moscowitz the placed resembled some sort of barracks more than it did a "home." Whatever it was, nobody appeared to be around.

"Hello…" Solomon sang to the empty room. "Chris…?"

A fat, haggard looking woman, who could have been anywhere between 40 and 70 years old, emerged from the shadows of another room and regarded Solomon with bewilderment, quickly hardening into hostility. Her drab house dress displayed large wet blotches; her large hands were still covered and dripping with detergent suds. She seemed to have been doing the laundry when Solomon arrived.

Moscowitz smiled uncertainly, held out his right hand and said, "Hello there. You must be Chris' aunt? I'm Solomon Moscowitz."

The woman's eyes widened for a confused instant, and then narrowed into an angry glower. Ignoring Solomon's outstretched hand, she raised her voice and said, "You not supposed to be up here. You go out. Downstairs." She moved toward him, almost menacingly, jabbing her pointed finger downwards.

"Hey wait a second," Solomon sputtered, holding up his hands, "I'm just looking for Chris."

"Chris? *Chris!* You look for Chris?" the woman yelled.

"Yes, Chris! I'm here to see Chris." Solomon imagined that this obvious misunderstanding between him and—he was still guessing—Chris' aunt would now be cleared up with the mention of Chris' name.

"Chris not up here," the old woman said—no longer angry, just annoyed. "She not up here now. *You* not supposed to be up here. You see Chris downstairs. At firehouse."

"At…what…where? *What* house???"

"At firehouse. FIREHOUSE!!"

The old woman gestured with her hands at the grimy walls around her. "This place is house for girls working at firehouse. You go there," she said in a tired voice, already turning away to resume her date with the wash basin.

Moscowitz clomped down the stairs and out the door. He looked around at the street outside. What he'd been far too preoccupied to notice on his way over, he slowly took in now.

Bars. Clubs. Dives. From one end of the street to the other, as far as the eye could see. Loud thumping music, bright neon lights. Swaggering foreign men of every size, shape, and description cruising up and down the street, their arms around flashily dressed, garishly made-up local girls.

Solomon's eyes came to rest on a particularly prepossessing place at the corner of the next block. Ear-splitting music was issuing forth from it every time the door opened to admit or disgorge its happy customers and their giggling, clinging female companions. Painted a dull red on the outside, its sign read simply, **The Firehouse**.

Moscowitz's feet seemed to take on a life of their own, dragging him toward the place, almost against his will. Like a zombie he went inside, his ears trying to handle the loud music, his eyes adjusting to the swirling bright lights. A male attendant, perhaps the bouncer, took his bag and handed him a claim stub. Solomon stood near the door for a moment, trying to get his bearings. He looked around, wide-eyed and open-mouthed.

It vaguely occurred to him that under different circumstances he might have enjoyed this. A carnival of young women. Young women everywhere, most of them gorgeous, dressed in almost nothing. A riot of women, everywhere his eyes alighted. Lithe, dark, exotic looking, and wild. Young women gyrating on stage. Young women sitting against the wall in tight little groups, talking and smoking. Young women hanging onto grim-faced foreign customers standing at the bar, lighting their cigarettes and pouring their beer. Women dancing, yelling, whooping, and laughing. And stepping out, on the arms of eager male customers, into waiting taxis and hotel rooms.

And occasionally, Solomon now realized, into airplanes—to be the paid escorts of their tourist clients on resort islands like Boracay.

Elbowed and jostled at his place near the door, Moscowitz moved forward, pushed by the people behind him. His eyes locked onto the brightly lit stage as he moved closer toward it.

And there she was. Chris was one of maybe twenty girls on stage at that moment, a "shift" that had come on while Solomon was standing near the door. Her hair braided and her face more heavily made-up than he had seen it on Boracay, she was wearing a small, *very* small black G-string with straps that tied at her shoulders. It covered—just barely—her nipples, her crotch, and nothing else. Glistening with sweat, she was holding onto a brass pole, one leg raised, shimmying to the music. And grinding her pelvis into the pole.

Moscowitz watched her distractedly, almost completely disassociated. What seemed to fascinate him more than anything else at that strange moment was the expression on Chris' face. While some of the other girls on stage laughed, or made eyes at the customers standing at the bar, Chris' look was almost dream-like. Not happy. Not sad. But rather like she wasn't really there. Solomon glanced around the stage and noticed that a few of the other girls wore the same look.

After a minute or so, Chris' eyes seemed to wander, first toward some of the other young women dancing on stage with her, and then out toward the crowd below. It was then that she saw him. Chris and Solomon's eyes met. At first there was no response, as though her mind had not yet fully returned from wherever it had gone to seek momentary refuge. And then his presence seemed to register. She slowly stopped moving, letting go of the pole. Her eyes widened for a second; her mouth opened slightly. As the music pounded on and the other women continued dancing and gyrating around her, Chris stood motionless, staring unhappily at Moscowitz. Solomon stared back, almost paralyzed with embarrassment.

It took an almost superhuman force of effort for Solomon to wrench himself away and head for the door. He grabbed his bag and hightailed it from the bar, but not before sneaking one last backward glance. Solomon saw Chris watching him as he elbowed his way out, with an expression on her face that Moscowitz thought could be anything from sadness to defiance.

Moscowitz wandered the streets of Manila's red light district in a heavy-headed trance, barely conscious of coming to ground at a seedy little hotel in the middle of a rough and rowdy block. The hotel was conveniently sandwiched between a bar—where the young female doormen stood outside in sailor suits—and a storefront V.D. clinic. Solomon checked in, climbed the stairs to his room, and settled in for a long, *long* night.

Solomon was not all surprised at how little anger he felt toward his new-found dream lover, Chris. Instead, predictably, he managed to analyze the situation as a crime of stupidity, and then 'round up the usual suspects': Solomon the Space Cadet. Solomon the Stupid. Solomon the hapless *schlemiel*. Solomon, Solomon, Solomon. The smug face of his brother David—nodding grimly—came to him as he sat alone in his hotel room. Solomon went to bed and eventually slept, buffeted by punishing dreams.

The following day passed in a headache-ridden daze. By lunch time it occurred to him that, for maybe the first time since turning thirteen, he had forgotten to put on his phylacteries and recite the morning prayers. He could not make up his mind about whether he felt guilty about this, or liberated.

Day dragged on into night. Solomon ate dinner alone at a Pizza Hut, idly watching the garish crowds passing by in the street outside.

It was much later, lying in bed and staring at the ceiling of his little 300-peso-a-night hotel room, that Solomon Moscowitz decided the time had come to have a serious little heart-to-heart with himself. With himself, *about* himself. It began—inevitably—with the weighty subject of "Blaming Other People for all the Things About Myself that Really Piss Me Off" and proceeded more or less directly to such related topics as "Responsibility," "Maturity," and "Finally Getting Off My Ass." Three hours, two Excedrin, and a half a bottle of nasal spray later, Moscowitz was ready to relax and move on to the "easy part": the question of what to do about Chris.

Regarding Chris, beautiful gentle Chris, the matter was cut and dried. People do what they have to do in order to live in this world, in order to simply survive. And a few—very special people, indeed—manage like diamonds to dazzle and shine. Moscowitz lay alone in the dark and knew—knew more clearly than anything he had ever known in his life—exactly what he had to do.

Solomon Hersch Moscowitz, son of the late Harry and Bea Moscowitz of Long Island City N.Y., and Miss Maria Christina Elena Dominguez, were married a week later in a simple civil ceremony at Manila City Hall. The bride was beautiful in a modest but elegant white dress; her face radiant, her demeanor blissful and proud. The groom…well, the groom made a reasonably decent appearance himself, looking a lot better than usual.

When last heard from, the couple was living in Manhattan; the young wife pregnant, her husband doggedly attending graduate school at N.Y.U. Reportedly working toward a degree and a career in clinical psychology.

They are said to be very happy; the perfect couple. Rumor has it that the young Mrs. Moscowitz, although nominally Catholic, keeps a strictly kosher home and rousts her sleepy husband out of bed every dawn to put on his phylacteries and recite the morning prayers.

Brodsky in Paradise

I don't know why the hell these people won't leave me alone in the morning, or why they can't seem to grasp the fact that I'm just not going to be my cheerful, chipper, effervescent self at the crack of dawn. I mean, if I've told them once…

God, here we go again: one or another of these characters is standing outside, rapping his (or her) knuckles against my flimsy little bamboo door, pounding me out of another deep sleep, another rapid-eye-movement dream of my ex-wife Pam. A pretty good one too, as far as dreams about my ex-wife Pam go, in which she's got her long, svelte, olive skinned thighs wrapped tightly around my neck. Definitely one of my favorite ex-wife Pam dream motifs. The eight years of real, wide awake experience I had with those incomparable thighs—experience I can only dream about posted here, in this "grim outpost of civilization,"—almost makes it seem like the marriage was worth the aggravation. Almost.

The pounding at the door continues. I silence it with a noise from the base of my throat that sounds something like a pig's grunt. This, my first delphic utterance of the day, sets off my usual sunrise recital of roughly thirty seconds of dry, jagging smoker's cough. Which in turn announces to the village that I have finally awakened, and heralds the start of another working day. To be precise, my 916th working day in this lush tropical Pacific island paradise. But who's counting?

I rise from my rattan sleeping mat with some difficulty (I'm still sleepy, stiff from the morning chill, and about forty—all right, *fifty*—pounds overweight), slide open the bamboo door and instantly see my visitor in the dim gray, early morning light. As I slowly get my eyes pried open and my coughing under control, I stand there and wonder why I'm not at all surprised that my first visitor of the morning—up and around before the birds even—should be none other than Numero Uno himself, the venerable old patriarch and headman of this village. Yeah, this village, which sort of defines the word "remote," and where I have lived and "worked" for the past nine hundred and fifteen—make that *sixteen*—days and nights. But...who's counting?

My visitor: I really don't know how old this guy is, and neither does he. His children, grandchildren, and innumerable other relatives in the area like to say, and probably believe, that he's over 100 years old. I would peg him at around 70, 75 max. No big deal back in the States, but almost freakishly old for folks around here.

Looks pretty good though, all things considered. The light brown skin still taut. The old body still spry and muscled. The eyes and mouth on his dignified old face showing the traces of a million smiles.

Following custom and local etiquette, I usually address him as "Grandfather." His name is Ba-ba. (That's what I said: "BA BA"). Following custom and local etiquette, he usually addresses me as "Grandson." My name is Wilfred. (Yeah, that's right: "WILFRED").

This morning he has obviously decided to waste no time and to go for the direct approach. "Wilfred," he begins—and the way these guys pronounce it in the local dialect it comes out sounding like '*Wip-rid*,' "give me money."

"I don't have any money," is my clever retort, as I find my eyeglasses and slip them on.

"Wilfred, look at this. Just look."

He turns around, *drops his pants,* and shows me a skinny, old, almost concave buttock hosting perhaps the worst case of ringworm I have ever seen. Worse even than the one I've got under my left arm.

"Grandfather," I whine, "I really haven't got any money lying around the house here. And besides, you know they won't charge you for medicine at the Catholic Mission clinic."

He scratches his ass and says, "Money, Wilfred, money. The rice I harvested last season is almost finished. Soon I must buy rice, Grandson, *buy it*, from one of the stores in town."

This gets my goat, and I reply, "Grandfather, if you and everyone else around here would only pay a little attention to what I've been trying to teach you these last two and a half years, you'd all be up to your asses in rice now." As I fire this shot, my eyes drop reflexively to the old man's still-exposed buttock. He hoists up his pants with one quick jerk.

"Grandson," he continues, ignoring my little salvo, "at least toss me a few coins for kerosene, for cigarettes, for batteries for my radio."

"Grandfather," I start to say as I rummage around behind a moldering pile of old paperbacks for my cigarettes. I dig out my half empty (or half *full*, depending upon your point of view) pack of Camel filters. I light a cigarette as Ba-Ba grabs the pack, cops five cigarettes for himself, lights one, and gently stashes the other four in his rattan shoulder basket "for later."

With that he smiles, draws himself up to his full height and says grandly, "Wilfred, I'd like to stay around a little longer and chat idly with you about this and about that," he tilts his head from side to side as he says this, "but I have too many things to do. Very important things. See you later. Or perhaps tomorrow, if I'm not too busy."

Almost against my will, I start to smile as I watch him amble off. As much as these people can drive you crazy, it's absolutely impossible to dislike them, or to stay annoyed with any one of them for more than a minute.

Without so much as a backward glance, the old guy waves his hand in a final, dismissive 'so long,' and it occurs to me as he bounces off with his five cigarettes—*my* five cigarettes, damn it—that the chance to score those smokes was probably all he really came for. Well, okay: only 6:10 a.m., and already another satisfied customer. Jesus, what a job.

Having thus raised the curtain on another deeply rewarding day of poignant, heartwarming intercultural drama, it's time, as they say, to attend to my "toilet." Literally. I let out another few coughs, jump down from my doorstep to the ground, and proceed without further ado to a nearby thick clump of bushes. Shaded by trees. Nice and private. I yank off a handful of leaves—nice soft *absorbent* leaves, almost better than a roll of Charmin. I pull down my shorts, grab onto a handy little branch for support, and gingerly hunker down into a low, unsteady squat…

The last time my boss came through here—for a one-day visit about a year and a half ago—he spent most of his time following me around with a bemused smile on his face, shaking his head slowly, and making "tsk, tsk" noises with his tongue. He looked at my house, observed my daily routine, watched me waddle clumsily around the village. The whole day, wherever we went, all I could see was that bemused smile, and all I ever heard from him was "Tsk, tsk, tsk."

"You know, Willy," he said finally, "you obviously weren't born to this sort of life." Bemused smile. Tsk, tsk.

Well, I'm not so sure of that. Frankly, I have always believed we get the sort of life we deserve. And if we are lucky, *really* lucky, we get to live in a "present" that allows us to make peace with all the screw-ups we committed in our past.

I was born Wilfred Irving Brodsky, on the 19th of June, 1950, in Boston, Massachusetts. My father Julius was a taxicab driver; my mother Shirley was a hairdresser. My older sister Barbara was a pain in the ass. We lived in a dark rambling apartment on Morton Street, in the Mattapan section of the city.

Mattapan…Today, many, many years after the fact, I read that Mattapan—*my* Mattapan—was a "lower-middle, blue-collar working class, predominantly Jewish inner city neighborhood." Was I at all tuned in to this at the time? I guess. I mean, I was certainly aware that there were no millionaires, jet setters, geniuses, or Nobel laureates in my immediate environment; no brain surgeons, opera stars, or symphony orchestra conductors (although Mrs. Feinman next door did play the piano for me whenever I asked her, and someone—I never knew who—used to play a mournful bluesy saxophone, the low moans wafting languidly across a row of back yards from a nearby street). And sure, I knew from watching TV that there were a whole lot of people with more money than us, living in fancier places, dug in more or less happily in their post-war gothic, split-level homes set safely back on menacingly quiet, tree-shaded streets.

Once in a blue moon, we'd visit distant relatives (on my mother's side) who lived way out in places like that—people who sang opera, did "interpretive dancing," and always seemed to look a little vague ("soft as a sneaker full of shit," my dad would say in the car coming home). Or even more rarely, they would mount an expedition to darkest Mattapan to see us in our third-floor apartment on Morton Street, and would sit there looking distinctly uncomfortable, probably wondering if anyone was heisting their hubcaps down in the street. This sort of stuff I was very much aware of, but as for knowing that I lived in a 'lower-middle income, working class, inner city neighborhood,' forget it. How smart do you think I was?

Anyway, we lived in one of those classic wooden three-family houses—a big, dumpy, porch-heavy "three-decker" that practically defined the type. Six room apartment on the top floor, just the four of us. My father Julius, my mother Shirley, my sister Barbara, and me—Wilfred Irving Brodsky.

Don't ask *me*, incidentally, how in the world I ever got a name like "Wilfred." I mean, who the hell ever heard of a Jew named "Wilfred?" God only knows what my parents were thinking of, or why it never occurred to me to ask them in all the years I was growing up. Whereas they both now repose at the Agudath Israel Memorial Park—side by side in a lovely plot that I hope my crazy sister Barbara is taking care of, or at least visiting from time to time—I guess it's a little too late to inquire.

Our apartment. It leaked in a zillion different places, was arctic cold in the winter, baking hot in the summer, and probably looked a little like the set for Clifford Odets' *Awake and Sing.* I loved it. It was home.

The Yiddish word that pops into my mind at the moment is *"haimish."* The closest word for this in English, I suppose, would be "homey," or something like that, but *haimish* connotes a hell of a lot more: an intense, almost narcotic sense of 'feeling at home,' and never wanting to feel anything else. Our apartment was like that. Our street was like that. Mattapan was like that, at least until I was around ten years old. At that point, I began to suspect that another definition of *haimish* was "mind-numbing boredom."

But let's face it, when you're ten years old there really ain't a whole lot you can do to alleviate this boredom, this pediatric *ennui*, unless of course you're lucky enough to be one of those people who are regularly kidnapped and experimented on by curious extra-terrestrials. I wasn't. I was simply left to my own devises, in Mattapan. Thank God for the little things though: comic books, *Mad Magazine*, *National Geographic*, my trusty little transistor radio and, of course, TV. They all helped while away the banal hours and probably put more than a few worthwhile notions and information bytes into my impressionable young mind.

But probably the major diversion for me in those dear dead days, the one that I suspect planted the seeds in my psyche whose strange fruit I'm harvesting now, was what I grandly used to call *"The Voyage."* The Voyage, such as it was (I was only ten years old, mind you), began at the front steps of my Morton Street apartment house and proceeded on foot around the corner and down West Selden, to the very end of this long, seemingly interminable city street. From there, I would pass through a short side street which would take me out to the broad, scenic expanse of Blue Hill Avenue. Having broken through to Blue Hill Avenue—Jewish Boston's main thoroughfare, our Fifth Avenue, our Wiltshire Boulevard, our Champs Elysse—I would head south down the avenue toward Mattapan Square. Once there, I would cross the street at the lights and dip eagerly into a small but rather tightly packed little paperback bookstore.

After treating myself to a long, heady whiff of the scent of accumulated new Ballantines, Signets, Fawcett Crests, Pockets, and Dells, I would proceed to enter the store and feed my oh-so-hungry eyes. I looked but rarely touched. No one behind the counter ever bothered me or told me to scram—inevitable features of visits to most stores at that age, but they did monitor my transit through the store with a none too subtle form of corner-of-the-eye surveillance. So I made my slow, eager circuit through the shop, reading the titles, contemplating the covers, and just sort of taking it all in. I always tried to prolong these visits to wonderland as long as I could for two reasons: (1) this 'nothing' little store with its run-of-the-mill stock of paperbacks really fascinated the hell out of me, and (2) I was greedily savoring my anticipation for *The Voyage*'s next and most exciting leg.

Sated on the sight and smell of all those wonderful books, I would leave the store, cross Blue Hill Avenue again, and proceed directly to the Mattapan MTA station, where I would board a waiting streetcar. I'd pay my dime, get a transfer from the motorman, and find a good seat with a nice big window. The streetcar would take off, its wheels squealing, its everything else rattling, and rumble off away from Mattapan Square. We would fly (this streetcar was designated as a "high-speed trolley" by the MTA) through wooded back lots, over bridges, and into little pocket tunnels all the way to Ashmont Station. Christ, what a ride.

At Ashmont, the end of the line, I would switch to a beaten up, round-backed old bus marked "Norfolk." The buses, like the streetcars and the trackless trolleys, were painted in the MTA's colors of orange and silver. Again, I'd find myself a good seat by a nice big window and sit there as happy as a clam while the bus lurched off with an asthmatic whoosh, out of Ashmont Station, through the grim gray streets of Irish Dorchester, and on to Norfolk Street—the highway, as it were, to Mattapan.

The bus would spit me out at the corner of Capen and Morton Streets, where I'd hand the driver my limp, sweat-soaked paper transfer and triumphantly hop down off the bus and into a corner drugstore. There I'd cap my adventure with the purchase of a comic book and a request for ice water, proffered grudgingly in a conical paper cup by the sullen old biddy at the soda fountain. Then, back across Morton Street and up the back stairs to our picturesque little apartment, where more often than not I'd be greeted by my beloved sister Barbara, who—strikingly arrayed in bathrobe and curlers—would glance up from her *Seventeen* magazine just long enough to say, "Hi, stupid...Where ya' been?"

So, there we are. All of the familiar elements. Boredom with my surroundings, an evident preference for solitude, compulsive reading, a undeniable hankering to seek escape through travel, and total uncompromising disapproval from the women in my life. Seems I was basically the same guy at age 10 as I am now in my forties.

My nostalgic reminiscences are broken off in mid-thought. I hear a blood curdling scream from somewhere up the hill above me. Then another. And another. Jesus, what now? I grab my pack of Camels, jam my feet into a pair of flip-flops, and go bounding up the hill. Or what passes for bounding when you're schlepping over 250 lbs. on a 5'7" frame, with flat feet. I arrive wheezing and lathered with sweat (God, am I in crappy shape) and quickly survey the scene.

The entire village, it seems—every man, woman, child, dog, cat, chicken, and duck—are standing around and screaming at each other. At the top of their lungs. Hands flying, fingers pointing and jabbing. Combatants being pried apart by only slightly cooler heads. Yup, it looks like a major event.

Everybody seems to have at least a few lines in this show, and they all seem to be "on" at the same time. The men are yelling. The women are yelling and crying. The little kids are running around at the edges of the action, shouting out their two cents worth. And, as always, the flea-bitten, mangy little village dogs are barking and howling a blue streak. Who needs television when you're living with this?

Unnoticed in the hubbub, I quietly light a cigarette and try to make some sense of the drama unfolding in front of me. My comprehension of this Pacific island language is passably good—a lot better than my ability to speak it—and I think as I listen now that I can piece the situation together, above all the yelling and tumult. As usual, it's got something to do with money.

It seems that several months ago, Ee-ping (who at the moment is furiously, and somewhat theatrically, kicking dirt and pebbles in the direction of an angry knot of screaming neighbors) borrowed a certain amount of money (I haven't yet been able to figure out how much) from his second cousin Ee-hot (who sometimes brings me betel nuts from his garden up in the hills).

Ee-hot is pissed because Ee-ping hasn't paid the money back, "in all this time"—a phrase Ee-hot is repeating over and over again like some kind of weird mantra. The aggrieved Ee-hot is threatening the apparently insolvent Ee-ping with everything from lawsuits to sorcery. Ee-ping—defiant—is daring him to go ahead and try, while their wives are hollering and throwing what appear to be yams at each other. I love it.

I've got my arms folded in front of me, a cigarette dangling from my mouth—which I'm trying to keep from curling up into an inappropriate grin, and my prescription bifocal sun-sensor glasses perched rakishly on top of my balding head. Glancing sideways, I see that I'm standing next to a short, wiry old guy I like named Ko-og, who seems to have avoided being sucked into the general melee. At least he isn't screaming at anybody—yet.

I sidle over to him and quietly ask, "Hey Ko-og, how much money are we talking about here? How much exactly does Ee-ping owe?"

Ko-og turns toward me, his face set in a doleful frown that reminds me of "sad clown" Emmett Kelly, and dramatically quotes me a figure in the local currency—the sum total of Ee-ping's debt—that amounts to about twenty-five cents in U.S. money, at the present rate of exchange. A loud, involuntary snort comes bursting out of me like a bomb. I stamp out my cigarette, stare fixedly at the ground, and try to maintain a solemn demeanor by taking a lot of slow, deep breaths.

I live in a newly independent Pacific island nation and work for an NGO. The initials NGO stand for "non-governmental organization," which in this case is quite apt. No government in the world—no matter how incompetent or corrupt—would want to admit responsibility for me and my long list of well-intentioned failures. The company I work for, Transworld Development Concepts, Inc., likes to call itself a "grassroots, village-level economic assistance agency." They are headquartered in Washington, the "headquarters" consisting, I am told, of a lavish six room office condominium in a swank little building near the Beltway. I've never seen the place, and I probably never will.

You see, I wasn't hired there. I was hired *here*. In this country. In the small capital city on the northern coast. In a bar. A bar decorated with ersatz native spears, make-believe shields, and *faux* canoe paddles. Not to mention stuffed fish, cheap imitation 'kontiki' masks, and bamboo. Lots of bamboo. And featuring hulking, silent bartenders in washed-out Hawaiian shirts, and a handful of sullen young bar "hostesses" clad in black string bikinis and little white sailor caps.

I was hired in this fine establishment, at around 3:30 a.m., by the company's "Regional Field Manager," who, although not particularly tall, nonetheless introduced himself as "Stretch." Stretch Gordon, his full name. An hour or so earlier, Stretch had been deserted by his young "hostess" and had turned—drunk and desperate for conversation—to the equally drunk, somewhat portly little man sitting next to him at the bar: me.

"So, what'd you say your name was again?" asked Stretch, the Regional Field Manager, attempting to focus his eyes on me.

"Brodsky," I replied.

"Brodsky," he repeated. "Is that, like, your first name or last name?"

"My last name," I said, the old apprehension kicking in.
"You got some kind of first name there, Brodsky?"
"Wilfred," I said lamely, with my usual inner cringe.
"Wilfred," he mused, gazing ahead at nothing in particular. "You know, Willy, Transworld Development Concepts is always on the lookout for…ah…"
"A few good men?" I suggested, immediately regretting my sarcasm.
"Yeah, something like that," said Stretch with a belch, evidently missing the irony. "We're doing some goddamned important work in this goddamned part of the world. Hell, in this goddamned very country," he said proudly, snapping his fingers and waving whoozily at the barman, who studiously ignored him. Stretch lurched around and made one last futile ocular sweep of the place for his long-lost "hostess."

His eyes found me again and blinked open into a look of surprise. He asked me abruptly, "So what's the deal, Willy, you want a job, or what?"

"Huh?" I practically barked. "What the hell do *I* know about…I mean, you know, what the fuck could *I* possibly…," I trailed off, sputtering. I've always been amazed at how well I put myself forward, at how well I "sell" myself.

"Ah shit, Willy, it's no problem. You go out there, you move in, you show the goddamned flag, and you help our poor benighted brethren down the golden road to tomorrow, blah, blah, blah." He paused momentarily, I assumed for effect.

"So…what do you say, are you in?" asked Stretch as he signaled again for a drink, pounding an open hand on the bar this time. The barman lumbered over.

"What do I do? I mean like, what's my job?" I asked, warming to the idea.

"You'll be the manager of one of our field projects," said Stretch offhandedly, more concerned with a fly busy drowning in the glass of beer the bartender had just slammed down in front of him.

"Manager," I repeated, turning the word over in my mind, "Me."

"Yeah," mumbled Stretch, as he grabbed and lit a cigarette from my pack on the bar. "You."

Me. Good old Wilfred B., footloose and fancy free. On the run from myself after a quick but acrimonious divorce, career shipwreck, and a championship bout with depression (which depression won, incidentally, hands down).

I was in the process of drifting westward across the Pacific, in the general direction of Southeast Asia—Manila, Bangkok, and God knew where. Why

Southeast Asia? I'd heard the food was tasty, the women were gorgeous, and—after consulting my *Rand McNally World Atlas*—it looked as though it was about as far as I could get from home without leaving the planet entirely.

Seems as though some small, obscure part of my brain had taken over and was trying to steal a leaf from my old childhood book. I was attempting to resurrect the *The Voyage,* only this time on a somewhat larger scale. It had worked for me as a kid; it would work for me now. So, I decided to "extrapolate," exchanging my P.F. Flier sneakers for airplanes, and making the Pacific ocean my new Blue Hill Ave.

At the time I was hired, Transworld Development Concepts, Inc.—or "Concepts," as we call it for short—had two small projects in this country: an "income generation" project for coastal fishing families, and an "agricultural extension" project for a big tribal village in the hills. Of course I would have preferred the coastal fishing families, and cool breezy sun-soaked days on luscious white-sand beaches (not to mention therapeutic, restorative nights in the bars, with drinks served in coconut shells by hostesses in string bikinis. But unfortunately, *that* important project was "already staffed," so off went old Brodsky, up into the hills—grunting and wheezing every step of the way.

And yet, despite the drawbacks and disappointments, the drudgery and difficulties, I could nonetheless appreciate certain distinct advantages: A beautiful island. Pleasant climate. Great scenery. Nice people. Fresh seafood on the coast. A fabulous array of tropical fruits in the hills. New experiences. New acquaintances. Time for reading, writing, and reflection. And all this in a newly independent country *with no extradition treaty with the United States.* A helpful consideration if you ever find yourself owing a substantial amount of money in back taxes, alimony, and unpaid gas and electric bills.

Like I said, we get the kind of life we deserve.

The heat of late morning is extreme but soothing. Dry-season sky—eye-searing, blazing blue with barely a memory of a cloud. I take my ease on a shaded little veranda at the side of my house, working on a cigarette and pondering the imponderables. I wonder if I should head down to the river below the village and enjoy a short swim before lunch. Or whether I might just as well blow off the swim and move directly to lunch. I wonder also what the hell time it is, having finally broken my long-suffering Seiko wristwatch in a particularly clumsy pratfall a few days ago. To make a long story short, I fell flat on my ass and slid halfway down a very steep hill, like something out of a Saturday morning cartoon.

I glance up at the sun appraisingly, marking its transit and position in the sky. I make meticulous note of the lengthening shadows on the opposite hillside. I listen carefully for the hum of certain telltale insects, their presence or absence another useful indicator of time. Finally, I toss my cigarette butt off the veranda with a muttered curse and admit to myself that I can't tell time without a goddamned watch.

Someone calls my name. A woman's voice, from the other side of the house. My name again, louder this time, the voice rising slightly on the second syllable, as in a question. I yell that I'm out here, on my little veranda, pausing awkwardly before 'veranda,' trying desperately to remember the word for it in the local language. I hear some soft answering laughter and the shuffling of what sounds like two pairs of bare feet coming around the side of the house.

A woman and a small girl, mother and daughter, both lugging full baskets on their backs, the basket straps around their foreheads. My mood instantly brightens.

"Hello, Undang. A good midday to you too, I-ling," I call out, genuinely happy to see them.

"Good midday to you as well, Wilfred," replies Undang, the mother, as she and her daughter slide out from under their heavy baskets.

"Where are you coming from?" I ask, observing proper conversational etiquette.

"From our fields," she says, gesturing with her head back toward the hills above the village. "We thought we'd rest here and chat with you a while before continuing home."

Little I-ling plunks herself down next to me and stares at some scratches on my elbow, the trophy from another slapstick fall the day before yesterday. Undang stands opposite from me, both hands massaging the small of her back. The movement causes her tattered jersey to be stretched taut against her breasts. I hope she doesn't notice me staring through my sunglasses.

Undang seats herself at an angle to me, reaches into the little breast pocket of my T-shirt and grabs my pack of cigarettes. She reaches in again for my lighter. A bit forward for a youngish married woman; around here it's usually only little girls or wrinkled old crones that would do something like this. Undang appears unconcerned as she lights a cigarette and tucks one behind each ear, "for later." She slips the pack and lighter back into my pocket, blowing smoke and then flashing me a smile that accelerates my heartbeat.

I figure her to be about thirty. Four kids, still in pretty good shape. Very friendly, she was one of the first in the village to drop by and talk to me—or try to—when I arrived here and began to learn the language. Great sense of humor, sparkling eyes and radiant smile. Never fails to start a stirring, as they say, in my "loins." Unrequited, of course.

"It's hot, Wilfred. We've been clearing our field all morning. I'm tired."

"Undang, why won't you at least try the new gardening techniques I told you about?"

She says nothing, but gazes off in the direction of her fields in the hills, a faint smile playing on her face.

"Undang," I pick it up again, "with those new ways you could have a fine productive garden right near your house. You wouldn't have to drag yourself all the way up into the hills." I hear my voice and realize I'm *kvetching* again.

She puffs on her cigarette and nods her head accommodatingly.

"And of course," I continue (in for a penny, in for a pound), "if you'd all only make the shift to irrigation, and grow your rice in paddies instead of up in the hills, none of you would ever run out of rice or go hungry again."

"And if the poor bullfrog would only grow wings," she replies with that dazzling smile, "he would no longer bump his behind when he jumps from place to place." She says this laughing, patting her own behind. I see this and slam my thighs together, not a second too soon.

Undang nods slightly to I-ling. They both get up. I-ling stretches and yawns, Undang unties the drawstring of her basket.

She smiles at me again and says, "You know, Wilfred, if I no longer went up into the hills, if I didn't have a garden up there anymore, then I would no longer be able to bring you nice things like this…"

She reaches into the basket and pulls out a bunch of huge ripe bananas, a kind I've seen only here, with red skins. And very, very sweet. I love these bananas, and I'm about to thank her until I realize there's more coming. Undang digs deeper into her basket and flashes me a look that sends my mind hurtling back across a gulf of many years.

I suddenly see my grandmother in the kitchen of her Elm Hill Avenue apartment in the Roxbury section of Boston some thirty-five years ago. Her face beaming, she puts a plate of something—cheese blintzes, potato kugel, mandelbrot—in front of me and says, "Enjoy."

Undang has the same expression on her face now as she lays a big bamboo tube on the floor beside me. About a foot long, and as big around as my wrist. A container of something, one end covered with a piece of banana leaf. Undang and I-ling gather up their baskets, hoisting them onto their slender backs. We exchange parting smiles. They continue their long walk home.

Following local etiquette once again, I wait for the two of them to fade in the distance before opening Undang's 'gift' from the hills. I reach for the bamboo and remove the leaf cover. Oh, Undang, wonderful Undang, you know the way to my heart—through my bulging stomach, of course. The bamboo container is full—slatheringly full—with fresh, sweet wild honey. Hot morning gives way to torrid afternoon as I sit on my little veranda, eating red-skinned bananas and slurping down honey, as happy as a bear.

In moments of self doubt, or moments of boredom, I like to sit and contemplate one of my "business cards," which the company made and issued to me at the time I was "brought aboard." My official title of "Project Director," printed on the card directly under my name, is perhaps a bit misleading. I am in fact the *sole*, one and only, permanent resident staff member of Transworld Development Concepts' agricultural extension project in this country. Oh sure, from time to time they send me up a "Technical Consultant" of one sort or another, or maybe a "Logistics Coordinator"—I suspect in the hope that he and I will sit down together and try to figure out what exactly a "Logistics Coordinator" is supposed to do. But basically, I'm "it" as far as this project goes. The man in the field. The man on the spot. The man whose ass will be on the line if something tangible doesn't start to happen up here by the end of this fiscal year. That's when the "Regional Field Manager" will come out here to inspect the project, smile his bemused smile, and make those "tsk, tsk" noises with his tongue.

The crux of my job—our "project mission," as we say in the development assistance 'biz'—is to "extend, enhance, and improve upon the community's indigenous forms of agriculture." Whose idea was this? Obviously, not the "community's."

To date, I have brought up close to fifteen thousand bucks worth of plows, harrows, picks, shovels, sickles, spades, hoes, crowbars, thing-'m-a-jigs, what-cha-ma-call-its, tennis rackets and yo-yos, not to mention—the *piece de resistance*—eight monstrously huge water buffaloes to schlepp all of the above back and forth across the rice paddies that I'm supposed to persuade these people to build.

Persuading those eight hulking water buffaloes to come up here was a production in itself, let me tell you. Part of the way in a big open flat-bed truck over winding rutted roads. The rest of the way on foot, single file over steep mountain trails.

"Hup, hup," I yelled—like a *shmuck*—as we drove the lumbering brutes forward.

Hell, I even had to call in Transworld Development Concepts' "Logistics Coordinator" on that one, whose major contribution to the effort was to bring me a fifth of Jack Daniels, which he handed to me like the Stanley Cup when we finally got the *verkuckte* buffaloes up here.

"Here ya go, Willy. From the Regional Office. We figured you'd need this after your first day on a 'cattle drive.' How right they were, I thought as I grabbed the bottle and violently unscrewed the cap, my hands still shaking from the tension.

"And also, Willy, think of this as a little token of appreciation from *me*."

"For what," I asked, in the midst of chugging the whiskey down like water.

"For today," he replied, starting to guffaw. "Watching *you* trying to drive eight water buffaloes up and down those hills was just about the funniest thing I've ever seen. I'll cherish the memory for the rest of my life."

As "Project Director" of this important community assistance effort, I may lack staff—God knows I lack panache—but I do not lack companionship. One of my major problems with my ex-wife Pam was children. Stated simply: I wanted them; she couldn't be bothered. Never mind, I have more than I know what to do with here. Perhaps you've seen, in one of those wonderfully garish gift shops you can find in virtually any Chinatown in America, those statues of a fat, bald Buddha with kids climbing all over him? That's me.

The village children love me. Why not? I am a source of endless fascination, of living theater, of hilarious slapstick comedy. The kids never seem to tire of following me around as I drag my 250 lbs. around the village, waddle up and down the hills, and fall flat on my ass in the slippery mud. One child in particular, a strangely quiet little girl with hauntingly beautiful eyes named La-ling, has become my virtual shadow. Whither I goeth, she follows. Always a pace or two behind, saying nothing, just watching me with those strange big eyes. By now, she could probably do my job at least as well as I.

La-ling's almost constant presence is kind of a mixed blessing. There's something comforting and reassuring about having this silent little girl around. Having someone to talk to—even someone who doesn't talk back—always beats talking to yourself. But sometimes on a late afternoon I'll glance back at this kid walking faithfully behind me and get heavily, royally depressed. Before I know it I'm thinking of my maddeningly enigmatic ex-wife and the life we should have had together—the home, the family, the car, the *kids.* It's usually about then that I kind of gaze around the village, glance down at myself, and start wondering again if this is really how I want to spend the rest of my life.

There's just no end to the interruptions on this reflection-filled, lazy hazy, and very definitely crazy day. Seems we have a "situation" down on the riverbank, where two of the male water buffaloes I dragged up here have gone berserk for some reason—boredom, probably—and are in the process of trying to slaughter each other. I join the crowd streaming down the hill to the river. I take a look and there they are: two of our strongest bulls—*my* strongest bulls—butting their heads, snorting and grunting, and trying to gore each other to smithereens with their enormous curved horns.

A few of the braver, or crazier, boys and young men of the village are trying to stop the fight—or at least get the animals' attention—by pelting them with rocks and sticks. The rest of us just mill around helplessly, watching the action from a safe distance. Which is really the only prudent course when two huge beasts the size of armored personnel carriers—but nowhere near as bright—are busy running amok. I light another cigarette, turn away and walk slowly back up the hill.

I've decided that I owe myself a little treat. A little morale builder. A few "mental health days" in another locale. A brief change of scenery. Around the beginning of next week I think I'll head out of here and make my way down to the coast. Or to be more specific, to town. We'll call it a "supply run."

I'll spend four or five nights in an "air-con" hotel room, taking lots of hot showers, pigging out in restaurants, and doing the bars. Especially doing the bars. I'll go to one little dive in particular and look for that tall pretty girl I had the last time I was there, the one who likes jazz music and gets those cute, kind of interesting dimples when she smiles. The one with those marvelous sleek legs that remind me…yeah, that remind me of good old Pam.

And perhaps while I'm there I'll set aside a moment or two to sort of mull things over. To maybe figure out just what it is exactly I want to do. Stay here, move on, or go back home ("Hi, stupid…Where ya' been?"). Just a moment or two. Nothing elaborate. A quick brainstorming session during a few minutes of "down time," like maybe en route from one bar to another. Not that there's any real hurry, or any pressing need to make a hasty snap decision.

Life is long.

A Trip to Town

He squats by the side of the dusty highway, in blazing sunlight, in pounding midday heat. Dust drifts by in languid clouds, the heat rises from the road in shimmering waves. He has been here since morning.

He carries little with him; he travels light. He brings his betel nut and a bit of tobacco. A string of white beads and a couple of polished stones. A bamboo container holding 55 Philippine pesos with a creased and faded national identification card. Some small ripe bananas to eat while he sits and waits. He carries these things in a worn-out old basket slung across his shoulder. What else does an old man need?

His long gray hair is oiled with coconut and tied up tightly with a strip of red cloth. A frayed T-shirt covers his narrow back and chest; a frayed white loincloth girds his waist. This too is enough, always has been. Enough for those that have gone before, enough for his father, enough for him, enough for his only son. His son. The old man rests his face in his hands.

He hears a distant low hum coming from down the road. Faintly at first, but slowly getting louder. The old man stirs himself and rises, he unties and reties his sweat-dampened hair. The low hum gets louder and more distinct, heralded as it approaches with a cloud of yellow dust rising down the road. The grimy little jeepney[1] comes roaring into view, shrouded by dust and exhaust fumes. The old man signals, the jeepney stops to take him on. He looks for a friendly face among the passengers. Lowlanders, strangers. He sucks in his breath and moves to climb aboard.

---

1. Basically a Jeep, customized and enlarged, used for public transportation throughout the Philippines.

The jeepney isn't full but the slackjawed kid with the cigarette in his mouth and the peso bills creased and wrapped around his fingers tells the old man to climb up on the rear bumper and hang from the back. The jeepney smells of rotting fish, the kid with the money in his fingers smells of gin. The old man climbs up on the bumper and grabs hold as the jeep takes off and speeds away.

The driver jams a cassette into the tape player, the jeepney blares Filipino pop music as it rattles down the highway. The old man gazes off absently at the houses and fields. Broad flat expanses of irrigated rice fields. Water buffaloes. Dust and heat. People in their fields, surrounded by undulating waves of rice. Lowlanders, strangers.

The rice is high, almost ready for harvest. The rice is tall also up in the mountains. Almost ready for harvest. Far off in the mountains, home. The old man reflects for a moment, thinking how much he would rather be back there, how much he'd rather be anywhere than where he has to go today.

His face is expressionless, but the old man is afraid. He reflects on this too, and it occurs to him that he has been afraid of something, someone, for about as long as he can remember. Afraid of soldiers, of police. Afraid of ranchers, loggers, land-grabbers, squatters. Lowlanders, strangers. Fear of these people has been part of his life since the beginning, since before his beginning. It flowed in the veins of those that came before, in the veins of his father and his father before him. Only his son was different, not afraid. His son. A hot dry wind buffets the old man's eyes and face as the jeepney rattles up the road towards town.

The town. The place looks dead and empty at midday as they ride in on billows of yellow dust. A tired hodgepodge of shacks and market stalls, beaten down senseless by the sun and heat. The old man squints from the blinding glare of the sun reflecting off corrugated tin roofs. He smells the fish, dried coconut, and old wood smells of town.

A dog barks, a baby wails, a tape cassette player rasps weakly from an open doorway. The jeepney comes to a stop at the entrance to the town market, the old man climbs down and silently pays his fare to the smirking kid with the peso bills.

Slowly, laboriously counting his change, he stops at a stall and buys a small pack of sweet biscuits wrapped up in cellophane. He drops these in his basket and starts walking down the street. He passes a small knot of young men sitting idly around an overturned crate topped by an open bottle of gin and a plastic pitcher of water. They smoke cigarettes and stare sullenly through hard narrow eyes as the old man walks past. One of them, lean and sweaty with his

T-shirt bottom rolled up to his chest, throws his cigarette butt at the old man as the rest laugh and jeer. The old man quickens his step and hurries by.

He walks through the sweating sleepy town, through the market, past the stalls, across the dusty plaza to the town hall. He climbs the steps and enters the nearly deserted building to face a fat scowling man in uniform, smoking and reading a comic book. From him the old man learns that the story he has heard is true. Yes, they are holding his son in one of the jail cells in back. Yes, he was arrested for stealing a cow and trying to sell it near town. The old man asks if he may see his son, the fat man rises to unlock a door in the rear, muttering something about witnesses, hearings, depositions.

The old man walks down a dark corridor to the jail cells on shaking knees. The cells are dark and empty, except for one lonely occupant. The old man stands silently at the bars of the cell at the end of the row. His son sits on the floor, almost lost in the shadows, with his back resting against the rear wall.

The boy turns his head slightly to see who has entered. The old man sees that his son's lower lip has been cut and that his left eye is purple and swollen almost shut. They stare at each other wordlessly, then the son slowly hangs his head and stares down at the floor.

The old man edges closer, lightly touches the bars of the cell and attempts a weak smile. His son does not look up at him again.

The old man asks gently, "Did they hurt you?" The boy is silent.

The old man shifts nervously from one foot to the other, staring at his son with frank bewilderment. Finally he blurts out, "Why?" The boy lets out a long deep breath and says nothing.

The old man starts to speak again but his son opens his mouth to cut him off. His voice quiet and low, the boys says simply, "Go home, father. Just go home."

After a little while the old man reaches into his shoulder basket and fishes out the pack of sweet biscuits. He tries a smile once more and extends his arm through the bars to hand the biscuits to his son. The boy sits motionless, so the old man stoops and gently places the biscuits on the floor inside the jail cell. Then he slowly drifts away.

As he walks back out into the front of the building he hears the fat man in uniform telling two or three others what the boy had said at the time of his arrest. The old man hears how the boy had stolen the cow and had tried to sell it because he wanted a radio and perhaps a wristwatch.

The old man listens silently and then turns to go, to another walk through the town, another jeepney ride, and a four hour walk through the mountains. Home.

The Seven Uncommon sons: A Fable

Once upon a time, in a storybook kingdom, there lived a miserable old woman with seven totally disgusting sons. How this poor old woman managed to go on living without blowing her brains out, nobody knows. Because, sad to say, each of these full grown sons had a habit or mannerism more repulsive than the one before.

The first son, he should only drop dead, used to drool all the time—every minute, every hour, night and day.

The second son, may his name be forgotten, had the habit of passing gas, loudly and odiferously, whenever a pretty girl happened to walk by.

The third son, he should only be covered with boils, used to wet his pants every hour, on the hour. A regular "Old Faithful." You could set your watch by him.

The fourth son—and now it *really* starts to get ugly—had the unfortunate habit of emptying the family slop pails, the chamber pots, on passing clergymen. That's right, clergymen: priests, ministers, rabbis, nuns, monks, yogis, fakirs, imams, ayatollahs, shamans, witch doctors, whatever. He'd wait vigilantly out in front of the house for these servants of the Lord to walk by and, as soon as he saw them, would run over and splash the family's "nightsoil" all over them. A fine boy.

The fifth son? *That* shmuck actually managed to make the fourth one look normal. You see, Son Number Five's specialty was to pull down his pants on the spur of the moment and display his "private parts" wherever the mood came upon him—the post office, the theater, the public library, at his wedding, in the middle of his I.R.S. audit; wherever, whenever.

The sixth son, for his part, was absolutely beyond belief: this winner—are you ready for this?—used to plunge both of his hands into the back of his baggy pants, grope violently for his butt, and then proceed to squeeze his buttocks with a breathless, almost frenzied abandon whenever he heard anyone mention the word "the." You can imagine that conversation around this *yutz* was, by necessity, somewhat careful and guarded.

By now you're probably bracing yourself for the introduction of the seventh son, and wondering, "Could this one possibly be any worse than the others? How disgusting can a person get?" Well, the answers to your unspoken questions are "Yup," and "Very," respectively. The seventh son was the undisputed worst of the bunch. The youngest of the boys, he worshipped his six older brothers and imitated everything—*everything*—that they did. God spare us.

Although fully grown, the seven sons lived together with their poor, wretched old mother in a small cottage by the roadside. Describe the cottage? Why the hell bother? They lived in a storybook kingdom, so go open any children's storybook and that's what the little cottage looked like, okay? You know, thatched roof, big stone fireplace, big copper kettle, big whisk broom, big cat sleeping by the fire—the whole schmeer. The only difference between all those cottages in the storybooks and the one we're talking about here was that, on account of their various repulsive habits, our heroes' abode was a lot less appealing.

Were they happy? Well, yes and no. *Yes*, the seven brothers were happy, as happy as pigs in poo-poo you might say, quite content and blessed with a blissful ignorance of the world beyond their humble cottage. And *no*, the old mother was not particularly happy, for she was cursed with just enough sense to realize that her life with these seven brutes was a hideous burden—some kind of penance for a crime she had never committed.

Needless to say, this was far from the most popular family in the neighborhood. Folks in the area tried as best they could to avoid the cottage entirely, which often necessitated fairly lengthy off-road detours to give the little bungalow as wide a berth as possible. Inconvenient, but worth the trouble. Let's face it, if you were a pretty girl, would you want to have to hear the notoriously loud flatulence of Son Number Two? Or how about this: You've just been made a nun—you took your vows that very day—and now you're running around in your nice new shiny black and white nun's get-up, with one of those fancy things for the head that drapes down fetchingly in the back and covers everything in the front but your beautiful, beatific face. Everything on you brand new, immaculate, and smelling April fresh, okay? You want to get clobbered with a chamber pot, for christsakes, by that crazy bastard, Son Number Four??? Of course you don't, and neither did the neighbors, who avoided the little cottage and its colorful occupants like the plague.

And so they lived, for years beyond number: the miserable old woman, her seven revolting sons, and their thoroughly disgusted neighbors in the town, who continued to painstakingly steer clear of the little cottage by the roadside—even insurance salesmen, trick-or-treaters on Halloween, Avon ladies, Amway representatives, and those well-groomed, oddly dressed Jehovah's Witnesses peddling copies of *The Watchtower*. (Well, to tell the truth, a few Jehovah's Witnesses actually *did* show up at the cottage door with their dog-eared, moldy little copies of *Watchtower*. Nothing keeps those characters away, not even the likelihood—no, the certainty—of getting farted at, dumped upon, or having to watch one or another of the lunatics in the cottage do something so vile as to make them walk away nauseous or questioning their faith in Jehovah. Also, some guy from the local electric company would pound on their door now and again, usually early Saturday morning when everyone in the cottage was still in bed, demanding to be let in to read the meter. Nothing much keeps *those* wolves from the door either.)

But, of course, all good things must come to an end. One dark morning, the old fat, merry, jolly, kindly Burgermeister of the town passed away. No big surprise, considering his weight, blood pressure, and cholesterol count. The townspeople mourned their departed potentate, for he had been wise and just. To tell the truth, his idea of burgermeistering had involved little more than sitting around the town hall all day with his friends and hangers-on, partaking of huge rich feasts of roast goose, imbibing enormous casks of red wine, enjoying a few contented puffs from his favorite long-stemmed clay tobacco pipe, and then falling forward insensate onto the dinner table and sleeping for hours with his face embedded in whatever food was left in his plate. Which suited the townspeople just fine. "Getting government off people's backs" is not a new idea, and the townsfolk were quite happy to know that, at any given moment, their little glutton of a Burgermeister was most likely passed out cold with his face in a plate of leftover mashed potatoes and not puttering around the town with his nose in everyone's business.

So the old *chazzar* died and was succeeded by his eldest son, who had himself sworn in as Burgermeister at precisely the same moment the town hall's maintenance staff were busy trying to lower his father's bloated body from a second story window with winches, pulleys, and piano wire. It soon became apparent that, in terms of physique and temperament, the son bore little resemblance to his predecessor. Where the old man had been pleasingly corpulent, the son was skinny and gaunt. Where the former had been jovial, the latter tended to arrange his face in a sullen pout. As much as the atmosphere surrounding the older man had been brightened by insouciant merriment and raucous good cheer, the younger man's world was somber and dark. The festive *joie de vivre* of the father was now supplanted by the almost Calvinistic severity of his son.

Not that the townspeople gave a rat's ass about any of this. What began to tick them off was the slow realization that where the father had spent years cultivating a total, good-natured disregard for the town and every man, woman and child in it, the new Burgermeister appeared to be taking the job seriously. In fact, the boy's first act as "B.M." was to have his father's magnificent, great, venerable, old oak dining table—which could comfortably seat up to 200 really obese guests—taken out and replaced with a state of the art, snazzy new desk. The townspeople became apprehensive.

Yet their apprehensiveness was soon to turn to outright alarm as it became increasingly apparent that this altogether unpleasant young man harbored all sorts of new-fangled ideas about running the little town. Seemingly everywhere at once, the new Burgermeister would scurry about, poking his head into every shop and cottage. With this permanent look on his face as though he'd just tasted something really sour, he would go around clicking his tongue and scrunching his long nose in expressions of vague disapproval, while muttering barely audible remarks about "cost-effectiveness." "flow charts," "operations design," and the like. The new B.M., as it turned out, had 'been to school' and now worshipped at the alter of something called "Efficient City Management."

As each day dawned, the simple townsfolk were subjected to a fresh barrage of utterly incomprehensible announcements from the town hall. New projects; bold new initiatives. Planning. Systems. Development, redevelopment, demolition, reconstruction. Demographics and reconfiguration. Major public works projects; massive urban renewal.

It was this last point that had the bewildered little inhabitants of our storybook town especially worried. It soon became evident to just about everyone that the new Burgermeister, along with his rapidly growing entourage of technocrats and yes-men, had graduated with flying colors from the Robert Moses Academy of Urban Renewal, where they had majored in something called "Slum Clearance." There they had learned the esoteric concept of "eminent domain," and had mastered the arts of neighborhood red-lining, large-scale real estate expropriation, the mass mailing of eviction notices, rapid demolition, and the slow construction of highways and overpasses designed for speedy obsolescence. The townsfolks' apprehensiveness began to effect their sleep and digestion.

Well, most of the townsfolk. Back at the little cottage by the roadside where dwelt the wretched old woman and her seven repulsive sons, all of these sweeping changes, these dramatic new developments, amounted to *bupkes*. After all, aside from their other peculiarities, the seven sons were not what you'd call "overwhelmingly bright," and the old mother was sufficiently preoccupied just living with these low-lives and cursing her wretched lot. Fact of the matter was, none of these poor boobs had even the inkling of an idea that anything unusual was going on.

While the rest of the townsfolk were developing insomnia, stammers, facial ticks, nervous diarrhea, and other stress symptoms from the tumultuous events in the town, life in the little cottage by the roadside was pretty much business as usual. The first son went around drooling; the second son passed gas at pretty girls. The third son continued to wet his pants every hour, and the fourth son happily went on splashing men and women of the cloth with the family's chamber pots. The fifth son nurtured his habit of dropping his pants to display his genitalia. The sixth son continued to nervously grope at his ass whenever anyone around him mentioned the word "the."

And the seventh son? Well, he just went right on doing all of the above, more or less simultaneously.

But alas, these idyllic days with their simple pleasures were soon to end. For not even this family could remain untouched much longer by the tumultuous goings-on in the town. It wasn't much after the new Burgermeister began to settle in behind his snazzy new desk—with its state of the art computer assembly, networking modems, fax machines, video telephones, and customized Maalox, Valium and Prozac dispensers—that mounted town criers, their long trumpets blaring, began riding through the area bearing grim tidings and important updates.

"Ta-daaaa, da-da-da-da-da-da-tah-dahhhh," went the long brass trumpets; and "clippity-clop, clippity-clop," went the horses' hoof-beats as the town criers thundered through the neighborhood, bearing their bleak bulletins.

"Hear ye, hear ye," bellowed the messengers, "by order of His Excellency, The Unpleasant New Burgermeister, be ye all advised that soon to rise on this site will be a forty-storied, twin tower, combined commercial and residential complex, with both office and apartment condominiums, in a wide variety of floor plans and square-foot size ranges, with a three-floor fully enclosed shopping mall, six movie theaters, fourteen restaurants and fast-food outlets, and ample parking in a six-level underground garage. Hear ye, Hear ye."

"And be ye all further advised," the town criers continued, "that ye all have roughly one week, give or take a couple of days, to pack up your chattels, livestock, humble possessions and whatnot, and scram the hell out of here to make way for construction, not to mention the laying out of access roads and right-of-ways. Hear ye, Hear ye. Nothing follows; have a nice day," concluded the criers as they cantered off into the sunset.

Reactions among the townsfolk varied. Some people were dumbfounded. Others were bewildered. Yet others were in shock. There was a really hard-core group of people who were dumbfounded, bewildered, *and* in shock, all at the same time. One thing was certain, though: everybody was upset. Facial ticks became more noticeable, stammers more pronounced. Cases of stress-related diarrhea, already the cause of great general inconvenience, became more urgent and debilitating.

Back at the little cottage by the roadside, however, the scene was a little different. The seven brothers had stood uncertainly in front of their modest home, mute and uncomprehending, searching each other's vapid faces for some clue of what this dramatic announcement might signify. All except for Son Number Four, who had mistakenly supposed that the town criers were some sort of clergy, and had rushed into the cottage to grab a couple of reeking, medium-full chamber pots. Also Son Number Six, who had unfortunately noticed that the town criers' announcement had included three pronouncements of the word "the," and was responding in his usual unspeakable way.

As for the boys' wretched old mother, she had been inside the cottage, as usual, trying to clean up after these louts and had been far too preoccupied by this Herculean task to be bothered with trifles like town criers and momentous announcements. She did, however, manage a quick glance outside, and with another bitter sigh made a mental note to hose down the sidewalk, and maybe splash a little Lysol, around where Son Number Three was standing.

And yet, one by one, it slowly began to dawn on the members of this little family that something or other was going on. Son Number One stopped drooling long enough to notice that people around town were nervously blinking their eyes and twitching the sides of their mouths in weird, exaggerated ways. And Son Number Two's mating-call farts, loud as they were, could not drown out all the stuttering he was hearing, along with other unaccounted-for speech defects. Son Number Four's preoccupation with slop pails and chamber pots perhaps helped sensitize him to the fact that people everywhere seemed to be clutching themselves in the general area of their colons, and running around desperately trying to find unoccupied bathrooms. Something sure seemed to be up.

Something was. All over the neighborhood, townsfolk were talking. Everywhere you looked, people were gathering in tight knots on the streets, in the market, in every shop and store. Everywhere you stopped to listen, an incessant murmur, like the sound of water coursing through a rocky stream bed, could be heard. Frantic, desperate questions flew like missiles fired from a hundred different cannons, aimed in a hundred different directions. What are we to do? Why is this happening to us? Why must we leave our homes? Where are we to go? I wonder if the new mall will have a Bloomingdale's? And so on.

Meetings were held everywhere, in every house and cottage. People met over supper, debating and screaming around mouthfuls of food. The talking went on and on, the windows of every home lit up far into the night.

At last it was decided to make an appeal, to tender some sort of protestation directly to the Burgermeister. After all, people reasoned, his father was a lovely man (if something of a glutton), so how bad can the son be? Thus was a petition carefully drafted, and sent by overnight courier service to the town hall.

The unpleasant new Burgermeister, sitting stiffly behind his snazzy new desk, sullenly read the townsfolks' petition and carefully weighed his response. He vaguely recalled having read some kind of crap about something called "citizen empowerment" in one or another of those dismal textbooks he had had to buy for his graduate course in Participatory Management. Thus he decided not to dismiss the townsfolks' appeal out of hand. So, having angrily crumpled the petition into a tight, moist little ball, he now opened his fist, extracted the moist wad of paper, and pried open the offensive little document for another careful read.

After a moment or two of heavy breathing, gritting his teeth and flexing the muscles in his darkened jowls, the Burgermeister proceeded to dash off a quick reply to the troubled townsfolk. He thanked the good citizens for their interest in his bold new initiatives, expressed his appreciation for their partnership role in urban renewal, and proffered his hope that they would not hesitate to contact him again if ever he might be of further assistance.

"That ought to take care of the little fuckers," chuckled the Burgermeister as he handed the note to his secretary to type, copy, fax, and file. That out of the way, the B.M. rebooted his computer, clicked open his GAMES menu, and resumed playing *Doom III*, which was what he'd been doing when that insolent little petition had arrived.

As you can imagine, the Burgermeister's letter hit the neighborhood with the force of an asteroid—maybe even like the one all those pointy-headed, pencil-necked scientists say hit the earth zillions of years ago and caused all the dinosaurs to do their big disappearing act. If you can believe in any theory that neat. The townsfolk could not believe their ears when this crummy reply to their earnest, heartfelt appeal was read to them in the town square. Dumbfoundedness turned to anger, bewilderment turned to rage, and shock gave way to molten fury as the naked arrogance of the B.M.'s letter sunk in.

"Of all the goddamned *chutzpa*," the townspeople cried, as they prepared to march as an angry uncontrolled rabble on the town hall.

"Let's whip ourselves up into an unbridled frenzy," they continued, "and show that pathetic little geek what's what."

They gathered rocks, bottles and brickbats. They pried loose from the pavement huge granite cobblestones. They tied several lengths of rope into hangman's nooses. They lit hundreds of torches. They assembled carts and wagons, and loaded them with dried straw. They grabbed muskets and pistols, swords and cross-bows. They shouted. They snarled. They waved their fists. They exhorted each other on to greater and greater heights of fury. And then, having gotten all this out of their systems, having "worked it through," they dropped everything they had gathered on the ground—taking special care to douse each and every lit torch—and quietly went home.

In the days that followed, it was back to the drawing board. More meetings, more debates, more vehement arguments lasting late into the night. Everyone in the neighborhood was all too aware that the Burgermeister's deadline was fast approaching, and that they would soon be driven from their moderately picturesque, semi-charming storybook homes. Again, the questions flew: What are we to do? Where are we to go? Why is this happening to us? I wonder if the new mall will have a Radio Shack, a Magic Pan, a Filene's Basement? And so on.

It wasn't too long before some sort of consensus began to form. Following round-the-clock meetings and heated debate, the troubled townsfolk decided to elect a small but stellar delegation of neighborhood luminaries. This delegation, composed of the neighborhood's most distinguished citizens, foremost spokesmen and articulate advocates, would be duly mandated by the community to journey to the town hall, present themselves and their official credentials to the new Burgermeister, and grovel shamelessly at his feet.

As the townsfolk proceeded to appoint their delegates, a major problem quickly emerged: nobody wanted to go. One by one, various neighborhood luminaries were approached, and one by one, they begged off. This one was fixing a wagon; that one was thatching the roof of his cottage. This distinguished citizen had an ailing milk cow, and that leading citizen had a garden infested by thrips. This leading spokesman had a sudden attack of laryngitis. That articulate advocate had a mouth full of cold sores. Everyone and his brother seemed to have some pressing matter to attend to, or some grave medical condition requiring immediate hospitalization. One thing for sure: that new Burgermeister really made people uncomfortable.

"Ah fuck, c'mon guys," whined the townsfolk to each other. "Somebody's gotta go. So whozit gonna be, huh? Who?!?"

Well, dear reader, you know who. Truth is, you could probably see this one coming around three or four paragraphs ago, if not sooner. Almost *en masse*, the desperate townsfolk smacked their foreheads, snapped their fingers, hollered, "Eureka, I've got it," and turned their faces, their eyes and their hopes in the direction of the little cottage by the roadside, the home of our heroes. Where as fate would have it, at that very moment, Son Number Five was hanging his bare butt out the window, Son Number Three was striking the hour by wetting his pants, and two hapless Mormon missionaries were getting a surprise baptism from a brimming full chamber pot by Son Number Four.

So, with camphor-drenched handkerchiefs held firmly to their noses and mouths, several leading townsfolk paid a call at the cottage. They paused at the door, exchanging nervous glances. They knocked softly, getting no response. They knocked again, a little louder. The door sort of 'oozed' open, and they watched with barely controlled dread as the wretched old mother wiped two grimy hands on her tattered apron, patted her unkempt dusty grey hair, made some clownish movement that passed for a curtsey, gestured with a calloused hand toward the cottage's cave-like interior, and graciously invited them in.

The visitors shuffled in, slowly, hesitantly. They sniffed apprehensively at the fetid air. They stopped and stood just inside the door in a frightened little clump. They glanced dubiously at the furniture, and agreed to sit down only at the repeated insistence of their bedraggled old hostess. They gagged at the sight of the coffee she schlepped out for them, and couldn't even bear to contemplate the coffee ring and danish pastry she set down before them with a tired, raspy grunt.

"Yeah, well…let's cut the crap and get straight to the point," began one of the townsmen, swallowing hard and clearing his throat. But that point, pressing as it was, was quickly driven from consciousness as the seven sons began to emerge, one after the other, from the cracks and crevices of the cottage. The visitors stiffened, their eyes darting around the room. God knows there was plenty to catch the eye. Horrible sights—pants dropping, a mouth drooling, a chamber pot being dragged out from under a bed—wildly bombarded them, almost seeming to compete for their attention. But inasmuch as the townsman's last remark had contained two unfortunate mentions of the word "the," the first thing the visitors were really conscious of was the appalling sight of Son Number Six ecstatically squeezing his own behind…

Two days later, as the appointed hour drew near, the little cottage by the roadside was just a-buzz and a-twitter with activity and preparations. The seven sons and their long-suffering mother were taking their roles as the neighborhood's appointed delegates to the Burgermeister very seriously indeed. Arrayed in their best clothes and groomed to perfection, the little family was busy receiving townsfolk popping in and out of the cottage to offer last minute coaching, advice, and best wishes.

A grand carriage with six stately white horses, which several of the more prosperous townsfolk had decided at the last minute to spring for, pulled up to the door of the cottage. Everybody figured that if these *schlemiels* were going to the town hall as the community's representatives, then they could at least go in style. So, with all of the neighborhood's hopes and best wishes ringing in their ears, and with everyone's fingers crossed for luck, the poor old woman and her seven oafs clambered into the carriage. And with a sharp crack of the coachman's whip they were on their way, lurching off to the town hall and their meeting with the Burgermeister.

As they rumbled through the city streets, the seven men and their mother pointed, cackled, and blinked with wonder at the sights they could see from the carriage windows. Son Number Two appreciatively passed gas at all the attractive ladies. Son Number Five treated the town to the sight of his bare behind. A clocktower loudly chimed the hour, causing them all to glance reflexively at Son Number Three. Son Number Seven, meanwhile, was busy trying to emulate all six of his older brothers at once. And everyone in the carriage tried to avoid mentioning the word "the." In due course, they arrived at the old town hall.

The Burgermeister kept them waiting in his outer office for over an hour, while he sat inside playing something called "*Leather Goddesses of Phobos*" on his computer. The seven sons and their mother kept themselves occupied by leafing through all the professional management journals that were piled up and gathering dust on the end tables next to the sofa. The B.M. glanced at his Rolex and, with a sullen pout, clicked the "Hibernate" button on his Windows XP and buzzed for his secretary. After telling her to go into the waiting room and usher in that bothersome little "delegation" that had turned up from somewhere or other, he sat back in his Lazy Boy office recliner and mentally girded himself for combat.

As the pretty young secretary entered the outer office to tell the family they could go in to see the Burgermeister, she heard a suspicious sound. Something kind of like air escaping from the neck of an untied balloon. Or something like the noise her grossly obese uncle always made an hour or so after his favorite supper of beans 'n beer. Reflexively she sniffed the air. Never mind, she figured. Must be her imagination. She ushered the family into the Burgermeister's office just as the old town hall clocktower was striking the hour, and just as the town hall chaplain—the B.M.'s personal clergyman—was entering the office to recite a short benediction...

No one will ever know for certain exactly what transpired at that fateful meeting in the Burgermeister's office. Although you can probably guess. The secretary, who was sitting at her desk just outside the office door, later reported having heard shocked screams, anguished groans, a lot of gagging and retching, a lot of coughing, more anguished groans, and something metallic—some kind of pot, maybe—clanging against the wall inside. When the office door swung open and the seven sons and their mother filed out, all that was left to see was the town hall chaplain passed out cold on the floor—his clothes dirty, his hair wet and matted—and the Burgermeister, slumped back in his recliner, staring vacantly—his mind far, far away.

Within moments of the meeting's end, mounted town criers were once again thundering through the streets of the neighborhood. This time the news was good:

"Hear ye, hear ye, and oyez, oyez," bellowed the messengers, "be it known to ye all that His Excellency the Burgermeister, who to tell the truth ain't feeling so hot at the moment, has decided to relocate the mall, the twin towers, commercial and residential condominiums, and the underground parking garage to another, less inhospitable neighborhood. So you can start unpacking your chattels, livestock, and other *chazzerei*, and disregard previous announcements. We apologize for any inconvenience. Good bye and good luck."

The townsfolk, as was their custom, stood around dumbfounded, bewildered and in shock. Again, they gathered everywhere in tight little knots, and again the questions flew: What does this mean? Has our little delegation met with success? Have we won? What the hell are "chattels," anyway? Now where are we going to find a goddamned Toys-R-Us? And so on.

The seven *schlemiels* and their wretched old mother came home to a heroes' welcome. Everywhere they went in the neighborhood people wanted to stop, talk, congratulate them, or just shake their hands. Yes, that's right, shake their hands—even the somewhat questionable hands of Son Number Six. Why not? The boys and their mama were heroes. They had saved the community, had spared their humble homes, had driven away the bulldozers and the wrecking balls, and had kept high-fat, high-sodium fast food outlets away from their neighborhood.

Nowadays it seemed as though the family was everywhere you looked. People couldn't get enough of them. Invitations to dinner had to be made months in advance; a party was considered a total failure unless one or another of the sons made a hurried cameo appearance. Boy Scout picnics, church dinners, synagogue breakfasts, speaking engagements, and lecture tours—the seven sons and their mother were everywhere at once, in great demand, the hottest social ticket of the decade.

Not that they had changed any, or altered their bizarre personalities so much as one iota. They hadn't. Each of the sons still did what he had always done. If anything, their shining celebrity and social success seemed to be spurring them on to do their respective things more emphatically, with more gusto, and with even less inhibition than before. But now people were ready to see things differently. Where once the boys were considered "disgusting," "repulsive," "repugnant," and "vile," *now* people were using terms to describe them like "unique," "eccentric" "colorful," and—that old favorite—"interesting."

Which brings us finally to the moral of this fable, which is simply the fact that all people have value—no matter how repellant, no matter how bizarre. Every man, woman, and child on this earth has a role to play, a job to do, a hitch of time to serve. Each of us has a purpose. Each of us has a place.

Except maybe people like Son Number Seven. You know, the youngest of the sons who emulated his older brothers and thus drooled, passed gas, wet his pants, tossed ka-ka, exposed his genitalia, *and* groped at his butt, all at the same time? What can we say about people like this? Never mind. They are the exception that proves the rule.

Brodsky in Transit

Barbara Brodsky knew they were in trouble the minute her brother Willy came staggering off the airplane. No more than two seconds after lumbering out of the exit tunnel and emerging into the passengers' arrival lounge, Willy Brodsky displayed his usual knack, obviously untempered by six long years of wandering the world, at being the proverbial pair of brown shoes in a world of gray suits.

Waiting for her brother, hoping to catch his eye across the crowded terminal, Barbara instead had to watch him jab a nervous, meaty hand into his shirt pocket, come up with a pack of Camels (*Camels,* no less!) and light up with the abandon of a true addict.

Already exasperated, she thought to herself: *"Oh Christ, if that yutz absolutely has to smoke, why can't he least try smoking a low tar cigarette, like Doral, or Merit, or **something**?"*

Barbara looked at Brodsky—haggard, disheveled, and at least fifty pounds overweight—puffing away at that damn cigarette, right in the middle of the airport, and knew at that moment that this "coming home and settling down" idea on which her prodigal brother had pinned his hopes was just not going to work.

Frowning and slowly shaking her head, Barbara wended her way through the press of people toward her brother. Before she had a chance to so much as say, "Welcome home, Willy,"—or something to that effect, no less than three different people in three different-colored, official-looking airline employee blazers converged on her brother to "ask" him to "kindly" extinguish his cigarette.

Blazer No.1, a 30-something, handsome African-American male who somehow wordlessly exuded the words "AIRPORT SECURITY," drew Brodsky's attention to the twenty-odd "*No Smoking Anywhere Within The Airport*" signs in plain view around the arrival lounge.

"Welcome to Boston's Logan International Airport, sir," he trumpeted at Brodsky, who visibly winced. "This is a totally Smoke Free Airport!"

Barbara listened to the man's triumphant tone of voice and wondered if he was planning to complete the sentence with something like a "Halleluya!" or "Praise the Lord!"

Blazer No. 2, female, fierce looking, and from someplace where English is spoken as a third language, limited *her* communication to snapping her fingers a couple of times in Brodsky's face and then pointing to the nearest picture of a cigarette, entrapped within a livid red circle, with an equally livid red diagonal line running over it.

Blazer No. 3, female, freckle-faced and looking like a former Miss Florida, definitely won the night's award for "Most Multi-talented," Smiling at no one in particular, she managed to point to at least eight of the signs—moving her arm back and forth in an overhead arc—recite some FAA anti-smoking law in a nasal monotone, thank Brodsky for flying the Friendly Skies—and all this while holding a cellular phone and loudly chewing gum.

His flight-weary, bloodshot eyes darting around nervously, Brodsky took in the disapproving glances from other passengers who hurriedly skittered around him, and noted that there wasn't a single ashtray anywhere in sight. Not one. *Anywhere.*

Barbara finally reached her brother and threw a protective arm around his beefy shoulders. Brodsky, meanwhile, was making a big show of holding his cigarette out in front of him, pointedly avoiding any further contact with it, as though it had somehow become leprous or infected with HIV. As an added touch, he began to slowly swivel his head back and forth, searching for an ashtray with that exasperated, "what-do-you-want-from-my-life" look on his face Barbara remembered only too well.

After watching this performance for a second or two, Barbara—Brodsky's hard-nosed, forever-unmarried, and unapologetically crusty older sister—smiled her slow, sad smile and planted an affectionate kiss on her brother's cheek.

"Barbara," Brodsky began, with the same whining voice that had played almost constant accompaniment to the years of their growing up together, and that had driven their long-departed parents half out of their minds, "all of a sudden there's no smoking in airports and airplanes, and there isn't a single goddamn ashtray anywhere in the world."

Barbara stared at her brother for a moment and, more amused than annoyed, said, "No kidding, genius. Where have you been all these years?"

As far as his sister, friends and acquaintances were concerned, all that could be said with any certainty in the first few days of his return was that Willy Brodsky had been "away" for a little over six years. If truth be told, his sister, friends and acquaintances were of the general opinion that Wilfred Irving Brodsky, fat and fortyish, balding and perennially peering at the world somewhat vaguely through a pair of tinted wire-rim glasses, had been "away" for at least two years prior to actually leaving his cluttered little apartment outside of Boston and bolting the U.S.A. "Away" from anywhere or anything resembling reality—*that* was for sure, schlepping around like a zombie, going through the motions of living a life.

Once, Brodsky had been gainfully employed as a reasonably proficient writer of advertising blurb for a publisher of industrial trade magazines, a job he had fallen into—like a mastodon into a tar pit—right after graduating college.

Once, Brodsky had been married, to an stunning young woman named Pamela—cool, svelte, and roughly half a head taller than he—who had spent most of their marriage trying desperately to remember, as she so often put it, 'just *what* the *hell* she could *possibly* have been *thinking* of' when she agreed to marry him.

Brodsky could no longer say with conviction which had started to unravel first, his marriage or his job. It was enough to remember that they both had somehow managed to implode and crumble at exactly the same time. Pam had walked out, wanting not so much as a coffee mug as a souvenir of their eight-year marriage; and Brodsky had stomped out of his job at the publisher, spitefully helping himself to a boxload of office supplies on his way out the door.

Brodsky spent the succeeding months alone in his apartment, sleeping through the days, sitting up at night, devouring paperback novels while watching TV, eating like a maniac, smoking like an active volcano, and drinking like there was no tomorrow. He was aware that, in a perverse way, he was having the time of his life.

Several months of this, though, and Brodsky began to make some disturbing observations. For one, he noticed that he'd grown so fat eating hot-dogs, hamburgers, submarine sandwiches, hot oven grinders, Stovetop Stuffing, Hamburger Helper, Kraft Macaroni and Cheese, Chef Boyardee Meat Ravioli, French's Instant Mashed Potatoes with Franco-American Chicken Gravy,

Frito's Corn Chips, Pringle's Sour Cream and Onion Potato Chips, Oreo Cookies, Wingdings, Ding Dongs, Devil Dogs and Captain Crunch Cereal, not to mention Hiram Walker Ten-High Whiskey and a nightly six-pack of Lite Beer from Miller, that he could no longer tie the draw string of the terrycloth bathrobe he wore round the clock, or fit into any of his already severely stretched boxer style undershorts.

For another, on at least two occasions he found himself halfway through a Stephen King novel before realizing he had read it the week before. And for yet another, he noticed that no one, with the inevitable, indefatigable exception of his older sister Barbara, was bothering to call him anymore.

Not even telemarketing salesmen.

Not even wrong numbers.

Not even the collection agency charged with recovering all or part of his college loan payments. When *those* guys stopped calling, Brodsky called the phone company to find out if his line was still connected.

After a full consideration and in-depth analysis of these sundry indications of *malaise*, Brodsky came to a quick and rather surprising decision. He shaved, showered, and rummaged around in his closet for something, anything, that still fit him. He waddled out of his apartment, squeezed behind the wheel of his eight year old Toyota Tercel, and drove over to his branch of the Bank of Boston. After cleaning out his savings account and converting the cash to American Express Traveler's Cheques, he went directly to a travel agency that he and his former wife Pam had used to chart their honeymoon in the Bahamas and, with virtually no fanfare, plunked down a little over $800.00 for a one way air ticket to Bangkok, Thailand.

Why Thailand? Brodsky didn't know exactly. Except for the fact that he had eaten in Thai restaurants and liked the food, had ogled the Thai waitresses and found them very attractive, and had glanced at a map of the world in the travel agent's office and decided that Thailand was about as far as he could go from where he was at that moment.

About two months later, his frantic sister Barbara, half crazy from worry, received a postcard from Brodsky with a picture of an elephant silhouetted against a golden sunset, from someplace called Chiang Mai.

Now, with him back home—or rather in his sister Barbara's home, a one bedroom apartment in a concrete box of 12 identical such apartments, just a stone's throw from the Southeast Expressway in a drab suburb of Boston—the pieces of 'The Voyages of Brodsky' began slowly coming together.

Planted like a tree in Barbara's Ethan Allen recliner about two feet away from the TV, Brodsky would occasionally turn his head back somewhat toward Barbara on the sofa and relate a quick 'incident of travel,' usually during a station break or commercial. The easy chair would groan and wobble under his weight as Brodsky shifted to crane his neck and deliver his travel anecdotes—invariably presented in a rumbling, phlegmy baritone, with a cigarette bouncing up and down in his heavy lips.

It didn't take more than a day or two of this to start driving Barbara crazy. But at least she was able to start figuring out where Brodsky had been all this time, and what he'd been doing.

Something about teaching English to some tribe called the Hmong in a refugee camp in Thailand. Nine months or so of that.

Stories about the girlie bars of Bangkok. He related these with authority, like some sort of 'consumer's guide.'

A mention or two about "hanging out for a while" in Laos, looking for a job. Another stretch in Thailand, apparently, trying to earn enough money to get *back* to Laos.

Four-plus years on some island in the middle of the Pacific, working for some 'save the world' outfit, teaching the natives how to make rice paddies and plant "compost-enriched" vegetable gardens. (*"Where the hell did my brother learn about stuff like that, growing up around Blue Hill Avenue?!?,"* Barbara wondered to herself).

Back to Thailand and another job teaching English.

More war stories from the girlie bars in Bangkok.

Finally, some hazy, dreamy reminiscences of a couple of months lying on a beach somewhere called "Phuket"—which was exactly what Barbara felt like saying after four or five days of Brodsky's impromptu, over-the-shoulder travelogues.

Brodsky was obviously agitated. The smoking alone was evidence enough of that. It had been years since Barbara had seen anyone chain smoke like this, lighting new cigarettes from the smoldering butts of the old ones.

His drinking was yet another clue. Within four days after his return, Brodsky had managed to clean out everything on his sister's liquor shelf, including the 12 year-old, unopened bottle of Grande Marnier that one of her girlfriends and brought her from a vacation in St. Thomas. Barbara had noted with further annoyance that her half-full bottle of Bailey's Irish Cream, which Barbara would lovingly take down and savor on birthdays and New Years, had been among the first bottles to wind up empty and in the trash.

Not wanting to pry, Barbara silently racked her brains trying to come up with an explanation for what she was looking at. One of her friends at work had helpfully mentioned something about "reverse culture shock," and said her brother Willy was probably having trouble "readapting" to America and "reintegrating" with his former life. Which made Barbara think back to Brodsky's former life and wonder, *"Jesus, what was to 'reintegrate' with?"*

It was at some point at the end of Brodsky's first week home, while he sat glued to the easy chair in front of the six o'clock local news, that Barbara decided to try her luck and reach out to her brother.

"What's the matter, Willy?" she began hopefully, placing her hand on his shoulder. "Do you maybe feel like talking a little?"

Over the top of Brodsky's balding head, Barbara's eye was caught by a story on the local news about some "Good Samaritan" who had stopped on the Massachusetts Turnpike to come to the aid of a couple of guys in a disabled vehicle. No sooner had the Samaritan gotten out of his car, walked over to the guys and asked what he could do to help, the guys stabbed the Samaritan, kicked him unconscious while he lay bleeding on the ground, helped themselves to his wallet, grabbed his car keys, and then sped off in the Samaritan's car. Leaving him lying in a pool of his own blood by the side of the highway. Leaving him for dead. The video showed the guys, arrested and handcuffed, their faces...*expressionless*.

Barbara shrugged her shoulders and started to tell Brodsky that this was maybe the third or fourth story of this type she had seen on the news so far this year—poor schnooks getting whacked on the highway by the very people they had stopped to help—when she glanced down at her brother and abruptly stopped talking. Brodsky was gaping at the TV, slowly shaking his head. His hands, she noticed, were gripping the arms of her recliner, his knuckles showing white.

Barbara awoke the following morning to the loud crunching noises of Brodsky wolfing down a bowl of her shredded wheat, his substantial presence almost completely hidden behind an open *Boston Globe*. Barbara could see just enough of her brother to notice he was wearing one of her bathrobes.

"Barbara, listen to this," he rumbled by way of greeting, without emerging from behind the newspaper. "A sixteen year-old girl in Woburn...where the hell is 'Woburn'?—North Shore somewhere, right?" Still crunching away at his cereal, Brodsky continued reading.

"Anyway, a sixteen year-old high school girl was 'seriously injured' last night, picking up what she thought was a rock that someone saw fit to heave through the picture window of her family's typical little suburban home. This, incidentally, was while she and said family were *sitting there*, right in the goddamned living room, watching *Dharma and Greg* on TV. The 'rock' turned out to be some kind of bomb, maybe a grenade, which blew off her right hand. 'The police have no suspects or motive.' Nice, huh? *Oy.*"

"Willy...," Barbara gently started to speak.

"And get a load of *this*..." Brodsky soldiered on, "'A drive-by shooting on Nightingale Street in Dorchester'—*Nightingale* Street, Barbara! That's where Grandma's shul used to be, remember?—'left two people dead and two others wounded. A 'boundary dispute' over two drug dealers' territories is suspected as the cause of the shooting spree. The dead and wounded were all in their *mid-teens*.'" From somewhere behind the newspaper, Barbara heard two or three flicks of a Zippo lighter as Brodsky nervously lit a cigarette. Smoke rose from behind the paper like a distress signal.

"What's the matter with you, Willy?" Barbara addressed the open *Boston Globe*, aware that she was becoming rather annoyed. "You're starting to sound like crime was *invented* while you were away. First of all, you weren't gone *that* long. I mean, it's not like you grew up as one of the kids on the *Ozzie and Harriet* show or something, and then left America exactly at the stroke of 1960. You know, things were already pretty screwed up when you left. I mean like, come *off* it already."

"You don't get it, Barbara," Brodsky rumbled from behind the newspaper, his cigarette bouncing in his fleshy lips. "When you've been away—and a stretch of six years is nothing to sneeze at in the relentless march of American culture, kiddo—that's when you can really appreciate how much things have really fallen apart. The economy is in the toilet, the cities are out of control, some guy that looks and talks like Little Joe Cartwright from *Bonanza* is in the White House, and the price of a pack of cigarettes has gone through the roof. You got any more cereal?" From somewhere behind the newspaper, Brodsky shook the now empty box of shredded wheat.

Barbara sat down at the table across from the open newspaper, poured herself a cup of coffee and asked, "Willy darling, have you by any chance come across either the "Help Wanted" or "Apartments for Rent" sections yet?" She noticed a bit of an edge creeping into her voice.

"No, why? Are you looking for a new...oh, I get it," Brodsky mumbled, a little slow on the uptake. He dropped the paper, yawned and rubbed his eyes.

"Actually, 'Barbie Dearest,' I did see a couple of things—jobs in advertising, sort of—but both of the ads said, 'Women and Minorities are Especially

Encouraged to Apply,' so I guess we can rule out those." Brodsky lit another cigarette and coughed a phlegmy cough. Barbara gazed thoughtfully at her brother and wondered if, for purposes of equal opportunity hiring, *schlemiels* constituted a legally recognized "minority."

The following morning found Brodsky out and about, unleashed upon an unsuspecting city. Pounding the pavement in search of employment. Wearing a heavy gray wool suit he had left behind at Barbara's over six years ago, far too warm for the day's late April weather.

Barbara had found an add for an employment agency on State Street, one that promised to "analyze" and "evaluate" the applicant's background and work experience, "assess" his "undiscovered skills," and point him toward a "challenging, meaningful, and rewarding career". The agency called itself "People Power...*Plus!*", and its add hogged more than half a page of the *Globe*'s mammoth-sized Sunday classified section. Brodsky was skeptical and tried to pooh-pooh the add, but one look at his sister's face was enough to get him out of her bathrobe and into the streets.

Brodsky drove downtown in Barbara's Suburu—a twenty minute trip, and then found himself orbiting the downtown area in search of a place to park—a fifty minute ordeal. He finally declared defeat and stashed the car in what proudly passes for a parking lot in Boston: a small postage stamp-sized lot carved out of the rubble of a former building on the site, demolished some forty years ago to make way for "The New Boston." Brodsky shelled out fifteen dollars to the parking lot's drug-happy attendant and tried briefly to remember the building that used to stand there.

Brodsky found the building with the employment agency and squeezed himself into a crowded elevator. He punched the button for the twelfth floor with a pudgy forefinger and eased himself gingerly toward the rear of the car. The elevator was almost instantly packed with employees of the building's various high-powered law firms, cutting-edge corporations, and upscale agencies, returning to their offices laden with brown paper sandwich bags and white-domed styrofoam cups of Starbucks coffee.

Glancing nervously around at all the svelte, young, nattily dressed men and all the svelte, young, nattily dressed women, Brodsky realized with an inner groan that he was the only one in the goddamned elevator who wasn't svelte, young, and nattily dressed. Brodsky noticed that in addition to his unfashionable girth and distinctive *dishabille*, his hands were beginning to sweat like crazy—not "moist," not "clammy," but actually slick with sweat. This, Brodsky had long ago decided, was the bane of his life, diagnosed years before as an "extraordinary" case of "stress-related hyperhydrosis" by a much bemused dermatologist that Brodsky had consulted while still in college. Brodsky glanced around again at 'the Young and the Natty' and attempted to inconspicuously wipe his hands on his gray woolen pants.

The elevator opened on Twelve to a jungle of ferns, rhododendrons, and other large potted plants. Brodsky stepped into the heavily forested reception area and sank into deep shag carpet. A very young woman with a face like a painted porcelain doll eyed him quizzically, listened to him mumble something about a job, and indicated with one flick of her gold-braceleted wrist that he should take a seat.

Brodsky obligingly parked himself on a piece of high-tech furniture that looked like a cross between a train station waiting-room bench and something that hospital patients lie on while getting ultrasound. He grabbed the only magazine in sight, something about "Human Resource Development," and prepared to cool his heels.

And cool them he did, long enough to survey the scene. Brodsky returned the magazine to its place of honor on the little glass and chrome coffee table in front of him, wiped his lathered hands on his lap, and nervously watched the frenetic comings and goings of the agency's busy staff. Brodsky wanted a cigarette at this moment more than he had ever wanted anything in his life. He needed no signs or admonitions, however, to know that lighting up in *this* place would be socially tantamount to unzipping his fly and exposing his genitalia.

So he sat and unhappily eyed the men and women popping in and out of each other's offices. As the minutes dragged by Brodsky vaguely recalled an old *Twilight Zone* episode about a future "brave new world," in which people were forced to undergo complete physical overhauls upon reaching the age of eighteen. Obsessed with beauty and conformity, this future society allowed its young citizens a choice of maybe two or three alternative bodies and faces—a choice of two or three possible kinds of person for each young citizen to be molecularly transformed into. Brodsky goggled at the people rushing purposefully around this high-tech, fern-choked suite of offices and decided that the future is *now*.

The women—secretaries, administrative assistants, mid-level executives, employment counselors, resume and work experience "evaluators," career trend "analysts," and what not—all appeared to have been born at exactly the same moment, about 28½ years ago. All of them seemed to be trying to project exactly the same "workplace persona," while going for exactly the same carefully managed "look."

The men, somewhat older, around fortyish or thereabouts, looked even more to Brodsky as through they had all just rolled off the same assembly line. Same weird retro-chic haircuts, same light blue shirts tucked neatly into the same sporty light gray pants, same dark blue neckties, same narrow blue eyeglass frames, and the same hungry barracuda look on their still boyish faces. Not a hair out of place, not a milligram of fat.

Swallowing nervously and giving his hands another good wipe on his now soggy lap, Brodsky concluded that the whole mad retinue in front of him had been cut from two rows of paper dolls, one row of male units and another of female ones.

Brodsky glanced down at the dark wet splotches on his baggy pants, stood up and, without a word to the receptionist, promptly fled the office. His hurried departure occasioned no more notice or comment than had his unheralded arrival, some forty-five minutes earlier.

Lummoxing down the hall toward the elevator, Brodsky managed to collide headlong into a rising young executive bustling toward his office, obviously barrel-assing back to work from a power lunch. The rising young one dropped his syrofoam coffee cup, its fragrant, latte-enriched contents landing on the green marble floor with a sickening splat, spraying both his oxford shoes and sporty gray pant-cuffs. Brodsky cringed and stuttered a nervous apology.

The man stared down at the 'Big Bang' pattern of coffee on the floor with shock and disbelief. His face reddening dangerously, he looked up and glowered at Brodsky with undisguised loathing.

"You don't have to fucking knock me over, *fatboy!*" he bawled as he elbowed past Brodsky, punctuating his remark with one violent tug on the lapels of his sport jacket. Brodsky stood and watched the man tromp toward the offices of "People Power...*Plus!*", wondering which of the two of them was losing his mind.

"The beauty of this country," Brodsky reflected darkly to himself on his way down in the packed elevator, "was that there used to be room for different types of people. Room for the square pegs. Room for the out-of-place. Room for the wiseguys, wisegals, visionaries and slobs." Brodsky let out a distracted sigh and said out loud, "There used to be room for *me*." Startled, the people crushing in next to him in the packed elevator shot him quick sidelong glances and tried to move a step away. But there was simply no more room.

Brodsky decided to put off going back to Barbara's apartment. He headed his sister's Suburu in a general southerly direction and, avoiding the entrance to the expressway, wheeled around aimlessly. On a whim, he set a course toward Roxbury and Dorchester, thinking he'd take a look at his old neighborhood, the places where he had passed his childhood.

The neighborhood had obviously changed. Poverty lived there now, along with Blight, Decay, Hopelessness and Despair. Checking the locks on all four doors, he sped quickly through Grove Hall, where his mother, decades before, had thought nothing of leaving him unattended in his baby carriage outside a bakery where she used to shop.

He hightailed it down Blue Hill Avenue, the main thoroughfare of almost all his childhood memories. Streaking by Franklin Park and American Legion Highway, Brodsky counted no more than eight open stores or functioning businesses along the avenue.

Swinging onto Morton Street, he glanced quickly toward Lucerne Street, where two of his father's sisters used to live with their huge boisterous families. He was barely able to make out a desolate, burnt-out expanse where Lucerne Street had once stood. He passed the three-decker on Morton where he himself had lived, and noticed that the windows of the top floor apartment, *his* apartment, where boarded up with plywood.

Brodsky gunned the Suburu toward Gallavan Boulevard and wondered whether the country would be any worse off if Little Joe Cartwright from *Bonanza* actually *were* the President of the United States.

Brodsky returned to his sister's apartment a little after 6:00. Barbara was sitting in the easy chair in front of the TV, sipping a cup of instant coffee while watching an item on the news, something about a German shepherd dog somewhere in Rhode Island that had been found buried alive up to its neck. The news show's anchorman was providing voice-over accompaniment to the grim video footage, asking rhetorically what sort of "sick person or persons" could have been capable of such a "sick crime." Still shaken by the day behind him, Brodsky listened to the story with one ear, just barely hearing the word "sick" issue forth from the TV. speaker about three or four more times.

Barbara swiveled around in her easy chair and arched her eyebrows expectantly at Brodsky. One look at her brother's haggard face, however, told her everything she needed to know. The two of them just stared at each other for a very long moment, without saying a word.

Brodsky awoke the following morning to an empty apartment. After heaving himself off the sofa and launching into his daily morning recital of coughing, he wobbled around for a minute before finding his eyeglasses, cigarettes, and Zippo lighter. He lit his first Camel of the day and staggered over to the "dining area," where he found a note from Barbara, scotch-taped to the table.

The note, penned in Barbara's unmistakable scrawl, read: "*Willy—I had to run out for a while on an important errand. Fix yourself breakfast. Stay the hell away from the liquor cabinet. I should be back before lunch.—B.*"

Brodsky continued his performance of Smoker's Cough Symphony No. 4 in E-Minor as he lumbered over to the refrigerator. He grabbed the can of Chock Full-o-Nuts, scooped five heaping tablespoons into Barbara's electric percolator, and jabbed the plug into the wall socket. He scrambled three eggs, went rummaging through the fridge for a stick of butter, found none, and settled instead for a plastic tub of no-cholesterol margarine.

"Probably made from dandelion oil, or some other goddamn thing," he grunted as he spooned three huge chunks of the substance into one of Barbara's frying pans.

He sliced open two English muffins, smeared them with the margarine, and sprinkled them with a blizzard of garlic salt before popping them into Barbara's toaster oven. He made a low flame under the frying pan, watched the margarine melt, and then poured the scrambled eggs into the pan.

Returning to the refrigerator, he pounced upon an unopened brick of Kraft mild cheddar cheese. He sliced off about half of the brick, added the cheese to the scrambled eggs, and then tossed the other half on to his plate.

He opened the refrigerator one last time, peered inside tentatively, and noticed a half-full jar of tomato juice. He considered making himself a couple of stiff Bloody Mary's, glanced at Barbara's note on the table, thought better of the idea and closed the fridge.

He poured himself coffee, lit another cigarette, and went coughing toward the reclining chair to find the remote for the TV. The TV switched on to a morning talk show, which Brodsky decided to stay with, more for background noise than anything else.

He padded back to the stove, emptied the frying pan onto his plate, extracted the English muffins from the toaster, poured another cup of coffee into Barbara's monogrammed coffee mug, and hauled the whole *schmeer* over to the dining table in one awkward trip. As he began to bolt down his breakfast, Brodsky focused on the TV. The two "hosts," or "anchorpersons," or whatever the hell they were—a bleached-blonde, cheerleader-ish, girl-next-door type and a surprisingly sleazy looking, dark-haired guy—were chirping happily away about…popcorn. Brodsky squinted at the TV. and began to pay more attention.

First, he was treated to a couple of minutes of indescribably banal reminiscences from the 'girl-next-door' anchorwoman, about her being taken to see Disney movies as a little girl, running with her mother to the lobby snack counter and eating, as she put it, "oodles and oodles" of buttered popcorn. This sparkling revelation was followed by several unabashedly coarse anecdotes from her dark, sleazy looking co-host about his adolescent dating experiences in movie theater balconies. The show then broke for station identification and commercials.

Utterly mystified, Brodsky gulped down the last of the English muffins, wondering where he had left the TV remote. Before he could stop shoveling scrambled eggs into his mouth long enough to go looking for it, however, the show returned. The screen was now filled with the scowling, almost fierce countenance of a woman in her late forties, frizzy-haired and austerely bespectacled, whom the hosts introduced as a "prominent consumer advocate." The two hosts continued to gush, gurgle, giggle and chirp, but the earnest consumer advocate sat there glooming, as though she were about to announce that a *good night's sleep* causes breast cancer in males, and that it's the federal government's fault.

What the severe young woman *did* announce, however, was scarcely less astounding. Her face congested with anger, the prominent consumer advocate told a startled America that the popcorn they had been enjoying in movie theaters for years unnumbered—popped in coconut or palm oil—contained more saturated fat than a T-bone steak, two greasy cheeseburgers, four fried eggs, and God knows how many chocolate milkshakes, *combined*! And this, she added with visible rage, was *without* butter or salt!!! The angry advocate glowered at the camera and *demanded* that theater owners henceforth either use canola oil or start air-popping their popcorn.

Brodsky sat open-mouthed, trying to figure out what a "canola" could possibly be. He heard a key enter the lock of the apartment door, followed by the entrance of his sister Barbara.

"Barbara!" he barked, "the inmates have found a closet full of white coats, and they're parading around the asylum masquerading as doctors! What the hell *is* it with this country, for Chrissakes? Is there something in the air, or the water?"

"Willy…" Barbara began, putting her shoulder bag on the table.

"Jesus, Barbara. Who appointed these busybodies and *kibitzers* to be the guardians of the nation's colons and cardiovascular systems? What the hell gives these people the right to decide what I can buy, do, eat or think?" Brodsky was beside himself.

Barbara pulled a long white envelope out of her bag and handed it to her brother. "Willy," she said softly, her face spreading into her trademark sad smile, "happy birthday."

Brodsky stopped sputtering and stared dumbly at the envelope in his hands. "Wha…I…my birthday isn't until June," he mumbled, still staring at the envelope.

"That's okay, Willy. I don't think either one of us could hold out until then," she said smiling. Gesturing toward the envelope with her eyes, she said, "So open it, already."

Brodsky opened the envelope and gaped uncomprehendingly at its contents.

"An *airline* ticket? To *Morocco?!?*"

"Yeah, Morocco," Barbara replied. "Unless I'm mistaken, you haven't been *there* yet, am I right? Anyway, wherever you decide to wander off to from there is up to you. Just remember to send me postcards."

Brodsky looked up at Barbara, heaved himself out of his chair, and reached his sister in one leaping bound. He threw his arms around her in a tight bear hug.

Her eyes slowly filling up, Barbara said softly, "Who knows, maybe we'll all be a little less crazy the next time you come back."

Seventy-six hours, thirty-four minutes and eighteen seconds later, Brodsky was in the air.

Lovetaps

Face it, this is not a city for night people. Not like New York. *Definitely* not like New York, where a 3:00 a.m. expedition down Lexington Avenue to pig out on pancakes in an all-night cafeteria on East 86th St. could have you rubbing shoulders—and God knows what else—with as many people as you'd expect to see there at 3:00 in the afternoon.

Not like, well…Bangkok—which I weathered with wide-eyed, slack-jawed wonder after college as a Peace Corps volunteer—where round about 1:00 in the morning those lithe, feline girls dancing almost naked in the bars along Patpong are just starting to get warmed up.

And not like other odd places I've been to—not that I've been to that many—where even though things kind of slow down and chill out in that dead stretch of night between, say, 2 and 4 a.m., there are still all sorts of people out wandering around. Or out lounging around, over coffee and conversation, drinks and romance, late night snacks and cigarettes. All joyously savoring insomnia, or carefully nursing neuroses.

It's moments like this that make me conclude, once and for all, that *this* old town, this "City of Brotherly Love," more than deserves its crummy reputation. Check it out: no more than twenty minutes or so past midnight and I am absolutely, positively the only living soul to be seen. Maybe the only human being awake in all of Philadelphia. To all appearances, maybe the only one alive.

Not that I blame everyone for being inside, in bed, and as snug as bugs in rugs. This month of March came galloping in like a Siberian tiger—never mind the 'lion' crap, and this night is blustery and bitter cold. And this ripped-open, gaping raw chunk of West Philly between Market and Chestnut at 38th, where I'm trudging south and pressing against an elastic wall of freezing air, is a huge yawning canyon where the wind likes to swirl and howl. It's not a night for most people—normal people—to be out and roaming around.

It's a fine enough night for *me* though. Oh yes, yes indeed. The air may be arctic as I cross Chestnut Street and head west, pushing my bowed and bundled body against the wind like a sumo wrestler, but my randy blood is churning at a rolling boil. You see, I am in love. Or something.

At least I think it's love. But what the hell do *I* know? What the hell does any poor male slob really know, when you get right down to it? Whatever it is, it's intense. It's got me out here gleefully freezing my ass off, almost dancing my way down the empty windblown streets, and feeling like I'm walking on air. I couldn't be happier. I'm trotting over to see *her*, to be with her, to spend the night—hot damn!—with her, to lose myself in the rich opaque smoothness of her olive skin, the hypnotic pull of her black-brown eyes, the mystery of her faint smile, the vague but intoxicating perfume smell of her hair, her breasts, her…oh God. Be still, my stupid heart.

Really high-tailing it now, practically running. Sweating—actually *sweating*—under my hood and inside my thick knit scarf, I watch my breath make almost rhythmic bellows of pale grey steam. I must look like the *Broadway Limited*.

At 40th Street I dip south, barrel-assing toward Locust. I do two blocks of Locust Street faster than a speeding bullet and cross 42nd Street which, unlike its more famous namesake in New York, is at this hour dark, somber, and fast asleep. I hurl myself southward toward Pine Street, where I round the corner with an audible grunt of triumph.

Pine Street. *Her* street. I reach the middle of this tree-heavy block of solid brick Victorian houses, almost halfway to 43rd Street, and here I am. I glance into the little side yard between her building and the neighboring one, see a soft brown light in the bay window of her bedroom, and get a feeling like I used to get as a kid, riding with my family toward Palisades Amusement Park and seeing that fabulous roller coaster off in the distance. I decide to stop for a moment and try to compose myself—catch my breath at least—before ringing her bell. To hell with that; life is too short. Here we go. Right up the front walk, up three polished marble steps and into the old building's front entryway.

The entryway. I pause momentarily, to savor the smell. There is a distinctive, unmistakable West Philadelphia smell. You can catch wafts and drifts of it almost anywhere, but it tends to hit you most vividly in the entryway vestibules, front halls, and stairwells of these late 19th century buildings—almost all of them formerly one-family homes, long since divided up into apartments. It is a smell of old wood, old paint, old brass and glass. Old floors, old plaster, old moldings and light fixtures. Generations of lives lived within those old walls; old loves, and old lusts. One hundred years and more of dreams, joys, boundless hopes and unbearable sorrows. Of laughter, of weeping, and of long low moans in the middle of the night. It is a rich, lush, musky smell, and blended with the humid midsummer fragrances of dense drooping trees, rosebushes, flowers, and the sweat of hot still nights, it makes for something more sensual—more mind-numbingly, crotch-grabbingly sexy—than any other smell on God's green earth. A couple of quick whiffs and you're ready to make love to *mud*. Trust me on this.

The smell of the entryway on this brittle cold March night is pure and lacking most of the moist earthy additives it will acquire in just a few warming weeks, but it's enough. I reach for a small bank of mailboxes and doorbells, my dumb-assed heart pounding like a Cozy Cole drum riff, and press the bell under the little white card neatly hand lettered with the names **FITZGERALD/ LAVECCIO**. Fitzgerald is the name of the roommate. Laveccio is the name of my obsession. A name redolent to me of Sicily, Calabria, the sun-sparkling blue waters of the Mediterranean, and I guess of southern New Jersey, where she was born and raised. A name that sings and dances, that does the tarantella, and that conquered and occupied my poor defenseless brain like an invading Roman legion.

I stand there waiting, facing the locked inner door of the entryway. Simultaneously peering into the door's upper section of glass and trying to check out my reflection. I make a quick, last minute attempt to arrange my face into some sort of "attitude." Another futile attempt at the 'cool look' that has eluded me since the moment I first set eyes on this woman.

The entryway's inner door rattles with one violent lurch as she, Ms. Linda Laveccio, opens the door to her first-floor apartment down the hall. A grad school friend of mine once patiently tried to explain this phenomenon to me—why opening one door causes other nearby doors to rattle. Something about vacuums, air pockets, air currents, air *something*. Never mind; here she comes.

As she slowly breezes toward me to unlock and open the door, my Laveccio-addicted eyes greedily drink her in. Light brown hair undone and flowing down to her shoulderblades in shimmering cascades. The florescent light in the hallway playing off her flawless tan complexion, making it look perhaps a half-shade darker than it actually is. As usual, no makeup. As always, a pair of hoop earrings and a thin gold necklace glinting against the olive skin. The slender coltish body—just an inch or so shorter than me at 5 feet nine inches—improbably arrayed in a pair of tight faded Levis and a man's white dress-shirt, untucked and way too big for her (*whose* shirt, I wonder; it ain't one of mine). She looks positively stunning. I've never seen her when she didn't.

I take a second or two to make a quick study of her face. To check her mood, to get a sense of what kind of night this is going to be. With this woman, one can never be sure.

With *all* women, one can never be sure.

She jabs her key into the dead-bolt lock with her right hand and reaches for the lower doorknob with her left. The hall light is behind her now, and her face is briefly in shadow. She pops the dead-bolt, pulls the door open, and takes me in with—*what?*—an amused glance, or an ironic one maybe. I can't quite tell. Her eyes widen for a flash instant, the naturally sparse eyebrows bobbing upwards once. A gesture of greeting; one of her trademarks. She favors me with a faint half-smile, lips closed, one dark dimple slowly forming. She roughly grabs me by the collar of my coat, yanks me toward her and kisses me on the mouth, earnestly biting my lower lip. A quick taste of things to come. I can relax; everything seems to be under control.

Wordlessly she turns and saunters down the hall to her apartment door. I follow, hungrily eyeing her up and down. I follow her all the way through her apartment to the kitchen, unbuttoning my coat as I go. She stops at the doorway to the kitchen and reaches behind her to give my belly a quick, hard squeeze. Her hand travels down to the fly of my jeans and pauses there for an electric instant. She turns, wraps her arms around my neck and brushes my mouth with hers. I have just enough presence of mind left to notice that neither of us has spoken a single word. She loosens her arms, steps back and breaks the spell: "Give me your coat. Or are you planning to wear that exquisite garment all night?" she says softly, with that same half-smile.

I shrug out of the coat. She takes it and disappears down the hall with it for a moment. When she returns she silently runs her hand down my chest as she brushes by me. She opens the refrigerator, a bulky round-edged museum piece from the mid 1950's.

"Hey, Danny, think fast," she says as she tosses a can of Miller's at me—straight at my head—which I just barely manage to catch.

"Almost had you that time," she laughs.

She grabs a bottle of Molson's for herself, closes the fridge, and runs a hand back through her hair, which seems to part and flow around her hand the way water in a stream eddies around a rock.

"Where's Kathy?" I ask, suddenly realizing that I hadn't noticed the unobtrusive presence of Linda's red-headed, freckled roommate as we ambled through the apartment. "Out with her new boyfriend, that tall guy from the Psych department—Stuart something-or-other?"

She says this like a question, and concludes the subject of Kathleen Fitzgerald offhandedly, "I have the sneaking suspicion that good old Kathy won't be home tonight."

We take our beers into the living room, trading quips and making small talk through the last few minutes of David Letterman. Moments later, we are in bed.

The pale light of a mid-March morning wakes me up around 7:00 a.m. I am alone. Alone in the bed. Alone in the apartment. And, for all I know, alone in the world. I pick up Linda's lingering scent on the pillow case, on the sheets, and on me. Memories of the night come pounding back to me in brilliant scarlet. I hear myself now, almost purring like a cat.

Following normal routine procedure after a night with this woman, I run my hand languidly over my body, surveying the strains, sores, nicks and rubs. It is usually at this point that I flash on an image, a frequently repeated scene from the old *Star Trek* series—the one where the *Enterprise* has just been in a particularly bruising dogfight with either the Klingons or Romulins, and Captain Kirk is barking into his armrest intercom, "Damage Control, report!"

After a quick but thorough body check, *my* Damage Control reports the presence of a couple of angry raised welts on my neck, a darkening bruise on the inside of my right upper arm, and what feels like some pretty deep scratches on my shoulders and back. My left earlobe feels tender; my lips are swollen and raw. Yup, about average I would say, as these nights seem to go.

She calls what she does to me while we are having sex "lovetaps," and she was more than generous with them last night. I heave myself out of bed, smiling and feeling terrific.

I jump into my jeans and go whistling down the hall to the kitchen for a cup of coffee and a couple of pieces of toast. I find instead a short, curt note from Linda. It greets me brazenly, scotch-taped to the formica top of the table. It tells me to let myself out of the apartment as soon as I shower and dress, to avoid calling her or coming by "for a while," and to give her some time to "think."

I spend the following night frantically trying to call her. No one answers the phone. Doggedly I keep dialing her number at half-hour intervals. The receiver in my hand just rings and rings. Finally at around 1:45 a.m—almost the exact time that Linda and I had jumped into bed the night before—someone, thank God, picks up the phone.

"Hello, Linda?," I begin, almost mewling, "listen, I just wanted..."

"Dan, it's *me*, Kathy. Linda isn't here."

I feel a plunging sensation somewhere in the vicinity between my lower stomach and upper groin—I can't pinpoint where exactly—as my last remnant of hope hits the ground like a bag of wet cement.

"Not there? It's almost *2 in the morning* for Chrissakes. Where the hell *is* she?" I realize I'm whining.

"I really don't know, Dan. She didn't tell me. She just called me at work around lunchtime and said she'd be out, probably for the whole night."

I move the receiver from my right ear to my left and notice that it's slick with sweat. I wipe a very wet hand on the leg of my jeans and mutter something to Kathy about having Linda call me as soon as she gets in tomorrow.

There is a moment of silence on the line. Probably no more than a second, it feels like forever. I hear Kathy sigh, a long nasal exhalation that breezes softly through the phone line. When she starts talking again, there is an edge of sympathy in her voice that cuts through me like a razor.

"Danny, Linda's going away for a few days. To visit a friend in Princeton, and then a couple of days in New York." Pause. "She didn't tell you?"

"Friend in Prin...*No*, damn it. She didn't mention a goddamned word."

"I'm sorry. Really. I just assumed she must have said something to you last night."

I stand there like a dummy, almost fascinated by the sound of blood rushing through my ears. Kathy's voice comes droning in again, her doleful sympathy starting to get really annoying. "You know, Danny, it's not like she's never done this kind of thing before, right? I mean, sooner or later she always breezes back."

I start to say something, lose my train of thought, and decide instead to try to clear my constricted throat. Kathy tries a note of cheerfulness to fill the silence and gamely pipes in, "Hey, look. If I hear anything from her I'll tell her you called. Otherwise why not just call back again sometime around the middle of next week, okay? Dan...? All right?"

❊ ❊ ❊

Linda Laveccio. My relationship with this woman is multi-layered and richly hued. It is textured, variegated and complex. Not to mention intricate and multifaceted, enigmatic and many-splendored. Which I guess is just another way of saying that *I don't know what the fuck is going on*. Not with her. Not with me. And not with this relationship. About all I can say with any certainty is that I understand her even less (if that's possible) than I understood all the previous women in my life (which was practically not at all). It's been like this since I met her, almost a year ago.

I read somewhere, probably in one of those frighteningly shrill little self-improvement books one of my former girlfriends was addicted to, that we get the kind of love we deserve. There may be something to this. Allow me to introduce myself.

Every university in the United States has a hardcore, dug-in, and absolutely immovable population of poor lost souls. If you've ever been anywhere near a university campus, you've seen some of these people, I guarantee you. Unobtrusive and anonymous, this ragtag array of aging *schlemiels* seem to be almost everywhere, haunting the university like unexorcised ghosts. Holed up in neighborhoods surrounding the campus, they pass the years almost totally oblivious to the rhythmic waves of incoming fresh-faced undergraduates, who move in and, four years later, move on. They also have almost nothing to do with the bright young hotshots who fast-track their way through the two-year Master's degree programs and go on to bigger and better things. Except for the fact that not a few of these dear dreamy people *started out* at the university as fresh-faced kids or hopeful hotshots, years and years ago.

I'm talking about what I like to call *The Fixtures*—professional students, perennial degree candidates, graduate teaching assistants that time forgot, dilatory dissertation writers. Ageless undergraduates, eternal adolescents. Lifelong seekers of knowledge and "truth," refugees from reality, rejecters of the "rat race," bewildered hangers-on. All of them more or less permanent fixtures of the campus, as timeless as any gnarled old maple tree, carved stone gargoyle, or weathered-green statue of Benjamin Franklin.

The female specimens of this species come in two varieties: smiling, aging Mother Earth types in washed-out jeans or peasant skirts, wire-rim granny-glasses, little or no makeup, unshaven legs and armpits, worn out backpacks and Bergenstocks. *Or*, more recently, earnest lifestyle re-treads—wised up and on the make—formidably arrayed in dress-for-success "business suits," smart short frosted hair styles, designer eyewear, lots of makeup, lots of jewelry, menacingly thin briefcases, and spiky high heels. Who are they fooling?

The male specimens—far more numerous, incidentally—are more or less cut from the same cloth: balding, greying Peter Pans who know—believe me, they *know*—that the 1970's are long gone but can't seem to come to grips with this emotionally, or subconsciously. The uniform of *this* army has remained almost unchanged through three decades of campus life: long-sleeved plaid flannel shirts and jeans, or short-sleeved colored T-shirt and jeans (depending upon time of year). Tweed or corduroy sport jackets, faded jeans or corduroy pants, sloppy sweaters and worn out shoes for formal occasions and evening wear. Hair—greying all over and getting a bit sparse on top—still a little too long.

In all cases, these are people who, for one reason or another, simply will not let go. Just look around closely at any campus, you can't miss them.

Or should I say you can't miss *us*? Of course, I'm one of these poor schnooks. A member in good standing since...well, Jimmy Carter was president when I came here to start graduate school. Young, cocky, full of promise. Full of myself. ("Full of shit," as my older brother, a successful dentist on Long Island has almost gotten tired of telling me). God's gift to English literature. The ultimate, definitive interpreter of Elizabethan drama. The compleat gentleman scholar. Jesus, was I adorable.

The years went by and the promise slowly faded. I guess I just kind of lost track of the time. Ostensibly, I remain here to write my doctoral dissertation. *Madness as Plot Device in the Plays of William Shakespeare.* At the rate I'm going, this document will take longer to complete than either the Great Pyramid of Cheops or the Cathedral of Chartres.

Lucky for me, the English department has been understanding, kind—almost maternal. I suspect this is because English departments nationwide have always had more than their share of "Fixtures" like me to shelter and protect.

God knows, this one has sheltered me. To the point where I'm still given the odd Freshman Composition section to teach, along with the occasional night school or summer course. The money comes in handy: it's what I live on. The opportunity to teach now and again also serves its purpose: it reminds me I'm still alive.

So, enter Ms. Linda Laveccio. On the wings of my fantasies, floating into my life last June on a fragrant summer breeze. Exquisitely beautiful, and late for class.

My class. "<u>Eng.Lit. 106: *Survey of English Literature III: Elizabethan Period*; Summer Session I; one credit.</u>" Eleven undergraduates perfunctorily piling up course credits, dressed "down" for summer session in T-shirts, tank tops, cut-offs, jogging shorts and sandals. Revelling in the informality of summer classes. Pulling huge pungent-smelling hoagie sandwiches out of grease-stained paper bags. Eating them in front of me, cheeks bulging, lips smacking, and eyes glazed. Pointing one end of these oblong, phallic-looking things at me while they chomped away at the other, the contents of the sandwiches—gloppy tuna salad, mostly—oozing and dripping onto the seminar tables in front of them.

We were about ten minutes into our first class meeting, with me standing at the front of the room doing my usual introductory spiel, in my usual slovenly way. Leaning against the blackboard—chalk dust all over me—one hand resting on the chalk easel, the other running nervously through my thinning, greying hair. The door squeaked open, a indecisive second or two passed. A foot appeared, an arm slowly followed, and in she came. She handed me the "Instructor's Copy" of her registration form, her dark brown eyes scanning the room for the nearest empty seat. "LAVECCIO, LINDA. COLLEGE OF GENERAL STUDIES. SENIOR. MAJOR: undeclared." Blushing and smiling a silent apology, she softly hurried in and took a seat near the door. She blinked her eyes once or twice, her tan throat flexing once in a quick, nervous swallow. She set her bag down on the floor next to her seat, flipped open a thin spiral notebook, and clicked a ballpoint pen into action. With a gentle hand flourish of long graceful fingers she brushed her shimmering light brown hair back from her forehead, let out one last harried sigh, and looked up at me. With a slow, spreading closed-mouth smile.

I seemed to be the last person in room aware of the fact that I'd been standing there, my mouth hanging open, staring dumbly at this woman since the second she came through the door. Hit, as the Sicilians say, by "The Thunderbolt." The sound of people snickering brought me back to my senses. I was grateful I'd evidently retained just enough presence of mind to keep from drooling or licking my lips.

I somehow managed to get through the rest of the class, God knows how. As the students lumbered noisily out of the room, I tried to avoid staring at this

Linda Laveccio—this dream image come to life—as she gathered up her things and quietly breezed away.

Jesus, what a rush. I have almost no memory of what I did or where I went in the hours after class. Late afternoon found me wandering the floors of the main library—a hulking box of brick, steel and glass, an eroding monument to the prosperous mid-sixties with their rich university endowments. I wasn't kidding myself. I knew I was looking for her. My one hope was that if I found her, I could somehow manage to appear as though I'd been looking for—where the hell was I...the library?—well, for a *book*.

As I lummoxed my way through the building I began to realize that my chances of finding her there were maybe one in a million. Big place, lots of nooks and crannies. And who was to say she was even there?

Strange things happen, though. The Philadelphia Phillies win a game occasionally, the Democrats squeek by to capture a narrow majority in the Senate, you file a tax return and don't get audited. And a man searching for the proverbial needle in a haystack beats the odds and finds it. Just as I was nearing the end of my aimless patrol, I got lucky.

Heading for the big glass exit doors, I happened to glance at the check-out counter. And there she was. Handing her card to a lanky young clerk with one hand, and brushing back that shimmering brown hair with the other. I stood there and felt my throat constrict. *She* must have felt my brain waves or something, because she suddenly turned her head in my direction. She gazed at me quizzically for a second, trying to place me. She smiled in recognition—that mesmerizing half smile. I walked over to her, my heart beating eight to the bar. She was the first to speak.

"Oh *hi*. I didn't recognize you right away." The voice was creamy and cool. "My name's Linda?" she offered, saying it like a question.

As if I had to be told. As if I hadn't been silently chanting the name like a mantra for the last several hours.

"Right. Linda Laveccio," I blurted out stupidly, my head sort of bobbing up and down.

She gave me another quizzical look, which slowly transformed into that fabulous, knowing smile. We looked at each other silently for a moment, my face showing obvious embarrassment, hers amusement.

It was Linda who rescued the situation, pulling us out of the hole: "Nice class, by the way. I enjoyed your lecture. Stayed awake all the way to the end." Her soft laugh was musical.

"Thanks," I replied, "that's about as good a review as I ever get."

She improvised a make-believe frown and soothed, "Hey, just kidding, right? It really was a nice lecture, and it sounds like it'll be a good course. But…" She stretched the word out and let it hang in the air.

"But…? I repeated.

"I think I'm going to have to drop it." She let out a soft apologetic laugh, and made a slight move of her shoulders, a shrug.

"Sorry to hear that," I muttered, hoping I didn't look as disappointed as I felt.

"Yeah well, I'm carrying three courses as it is. Four would be a little much for a summer session. Too much for *me* anyway, that's for sure," she said as she flashed me that same vulnerable, blushing smile she'd given me earlier in class.

"What are your other three classes," I asked, desperately trying to prolong the conversation.

"Well, I've got a seminar in European prehistory, over at the anthro department. *Hey*, it sounded really interesting in the course catalogue," she said laughing, in answer to my raised eyebrows.

"And," she continued, "I'm taking another biology course, since I've always thought I might declare that as my major. And finally, an independent study in urban folklore. Left over from last semester. I'm supposed to take down life histories—you know, recollections from the old days, autobiographical stuff—from all these old Italian women in South Philly. I haven't gotten very far with it yet." She flashed me another blushing smile, and another shrug.

It occurred to me, listening to this and watching the body language, that I have met with *this* species in the academic menagerie also. The specimens, in my experience, almost invariably female. Bright but unfocused. Talented but insecure. Brought up to be bashful and deferential; to quietly assume their places in line, well behind fathers and brothers. Almost deliberately, systematically programmed to shun ambition and to lack self confidence. But beginning to chafe at the yoke. Beginning to rebel. Beginning to "define" themselves and wriggle free from their old selves. God help whatever man is around them when the yoke finally cracks. "God help *you*, you poor shmuck," a voice in my head softly whispered.

We stood there at the check-out counter and talked. The early evening onslaught of students heading home bustled and jostled around us, squeezing up to the counter on either side of us to take out and return books. We chatted on, oblivious. At least *I* was oblivious, to everything in the world aside from this spellbinding young woman with her cool narcotic voice.

What did we talk about? Everything. Nothing. You know.

In Philadelphia the month of June is like a small child petulantly demanding to being treated like one of the 'big kid' months of summer, July and August. We continued to stand there, talking and laughing, and after a while I became conscious of the fact that my feet were getting tired, my calves were beginning to ache, and that warm trickles of sweat were beginning to run down my back, beneath my shirt and sport jacket. I noticed it was getting a bit "close" inside my jeans too.

Linda, this marvelously surprising lady, came through again. Flashing me that knowing smile, she said, "Look, do you think we could take this somewhere else," she suggested, glancing at her watch. "Have you by any chance had dinner yet?"

I sprang for the bait like a hungry trout. "No, I haven't," I said, my heart racing. "Let me take you to dinner. Maybe someplace nice downtown?"

Her smile faded. She looked at me for a instant with her head slightly cocked, lips closed in a tight grim line, an eyebrow arched. When she spoke again there was something in her voice—an edge—that I hadn't heard before.

"I've got a better idea. Let's just go someplace around here. Nothing fancy. And we'll take each other, okay?"

Every "first date" has its hills and valleys, and I was feeling shot down and chastened as we left the library and cut across campus toward Spruce Street. Linda became quiet, pensive.

We wandered up Spruce and sort of fell into a little place at the intersection with 38th St. A crowded noisy hangout packed mostly with undergraduates, huddled over beers, grabbing greasy snacks, and playing the two blaring video games in the corner. It wasn't quite what I'd had in mind.

Linda and I each grabbed a tray from a pile near the entrance and dragged it sideways along the counter. We both ordered exactly the same things: cheesesteaks, side orders of french fries, and bottles of Beck's beer from a refrigerator case near the cash register. We found a table near the window, far from the madding video games, and began to eat in nervous silence.

The cheesesteak—pieces of chip-steak, onions, peppers and cheese, fried up on a griddle and unceremoniously dumped onto a phallic-shaped piece of Italian bread—is not merely Philadelphia's prime contribution to world cuisine. It is, quite arguably, *the* single most delicious food item ever fashioned by the hand of man. I defy anyone to come up with something better.

It sure did the trick that evening for Linda and me. A couple of ravenous bites, and we began to loosen up. The beer probably also helped a little. Her stunning dimpled smile wandered back, gently pulling my self-confidence by the hand along with it.

We traded life stories; hers set mostly in rural southern New Jersey, mine almost a cliche of suburban Long Island. She, the over-protected only daughter in a brother-filled, male-driven family of building contractors and construction workers. Me, the disappointing product of an upwardly mobile, upper middle class, very assimilated Jewish family. She, already 25 years old, drifting in and out of school, enrolling willy-nilly in courses that looked interesting in the catalogue. Finishing about half of them. And me, on the shady side of 40, a graduate student for life.

The evening gave birth to night, which dug itself in comfortably, and then slowly, gracefully grew old. All around us, people noisily came and went. The video games faded into silence, giving way to the Phillies vs. Atlanta on a ceiling-mounted color TV. I really don't think either one of us had any idea how long we'd been planted there, breathing each other in. A chubby young black girl, who looked to me way too young to be working, appeared in an apron to wipe the now mostly empty tables. We glanced at our watches—ten minutes to 12:00—and looked at each other with tired smiles. Linda raised both arms above her head, arched and stretched her back. She stood up stiffly, flipped her hair back over her shoulders, and went off to find the ladies room. I stretched, cracked my knuckles and thought to myself, *what now*?

Linda returned and stood by her chair, waiting.

"So, Miss Laveccio," I began, in my best teaching voice, "what's all this bullshit about your dropping my class?"

She smiled and said softly, "Sorry Prof, but I'm just not up to it. Maybe you could come and teach it to me privately."

"Okay," I said, looking right into her eyes, "when shall we start?"

"Well," she murmured, looking right back into mine, "how about tonight?"

My low rent digs in a rundown area north of Market Street optimistically referred to as "Powelton Village" were in no state to receive guests. My mind quickly flashed on the apartment as I'd left it that morning: a gaudy riot of unmade bed, linens and clothes tossed all over the floor, three days of dishes in the kitchen sink, a bathroom from hell—traces of a bachelor life that has lasted far too long to be picturesque. I felt a quiet wave of relief as Linda headed us west along Spruce Street toward her place on Pine.

A soft summer night. The air sultry and fragrant with the foliage of June, the sky a velvet black. At Pine Street above 40th West Philly sparkled and glimmered in all its summer night glory. The grand old oak trees lining the sidewalks were already heavy and bowed with their dark new leaves. The air was sweet and laden with the intoxicating perfume of a thousand lilac bushes in full bloom. Low shaded lamplight glowed reclusively from windows half hidden by trees. Snatches of quiet conversation; faint notes of music. Crickets and cicadas serenading the satin night.

The slender, coltish young woman at my side hummed softly, her hand resting gently at the base of my spine. I was already lost in love. Really, *love*. Pure and simple. Just like on TV.

We got to her building and entered the apartment, stepping lightly and talking in whispers. Linda's new roommate, a nursing student named Kathy, was asleep in her room. We continued down the hall toward Linda's bedroom, celebrating our arrival with our first electric embrace. Linda's hair had a scent of sweet jasmine. I had just enough of my wits left about me to notice details like this. We wasted very little time in shedding our clothes and sliding smoothly into bed.

What followed was wondrous and extraordinary. A true revelation, completely beyond my experience. Too intensely passionate to be called "sex." Way too hot blooded to be called "making love." Linda's transformation from cool young woman to what I was seeing now was amazing and, frankly, a little scary. I remember feeling very uneasy at times that night, wondering what the hell was going on. Was this love or war?

I was scratched, clawed, bitten, pinched, and pounded; pushed, pulled, and squeezed so tight I couldn't breathe. Bleeding, swollen, black and blue. I was stroked, caressed, massaged, and sung to—in a low soothing voice that gently tickled my ear. Hugged and battered, adored and assaulted. "Lovetaps," she murmured at some point.

This woman ran a range of emotions I almost could not keep up with. Moans and laughter, sighs and soft weeping. At times an almost detached amusement, as though a part of her had left her body and was watching the scene from a distance. At other times a seemingly desperate yearning, and an unreasoning fear of being left alone for even one moment.

The night pulsed onward toward morning. She kissed me softly one last time; we drifted off to sleep.

I awoke to faint music a little after dawn, Linda sleeping soundly, her back to me, nestled against my naked body. Birds began stirring in the trees outside, singing their songs in the gathering light.

Cooled by the June morning breeze gently fluttering the curtains at the window, I opened my eyes and let them wander. The time glowed with a soft green light from the clock radio by the bed. Music played faintly from a soft-rock FM station. I focused on the muted notes, trying to make out the tune. After a few seconds I managed to nail it, an old classic, one of my favorites. *From the Beginning*, by Emerson, Lake, and Palmer. I caught myself wondering how old Linda would have been when this track was recorded. Was she even born yet then?

As the song's last synthesized notes floated softly from the radio, I lay there and drank it all in. The song, the breeze, the sweet smell of lilacs bursting into bloom. The faint grey light at the window, Linda's soft slow breathing, the steady rise and fall of her breasts, still covered in shadows. The mind-numbing scent of her hair. I knew—knew intensely, in every nerve of my body—that I'd never been happier at any time in my life than I was at that moment.

If you're lucky—*really* lucky—some woman will do this to you.

❦   ❦   ❦

Cold windy March turns slowly into raw rainy April; dark crappy days fade dismally into long, grim nights. Still no sign of Linda.

I call her apartment every other day to find out if she's back, or whether her roommate has heard anything from her. After four or five of these calls, Kathy's voice on the phone seems to gradually shed its sympathy and pick up a distinct hard edge of irritation. I endure this a couple of times and finally stop calling.

I haunt my mailbox at home, and I visit my mail slot at the English department several times a day. *Nada*. I jump every time the phone in my apartment rings. Truth to tell, it doesn't ring very often; and of course it's never *her*.

My brisk, bracing late-night walks—little midnight "constitutionals," to "provide closure on the day," to "clear my head," or to "chill out before going to sleep"—always seem to land me on Pine Street. I blow by Linda's building—never stopping—and peer quickly but searchingly at her bedroom window. Once or twice I think I see a light showing faintly through the curtains, but I'm not sure.

Otherwise, I go through the motions of living my life. I get up in the morning and plod through the day. I shower, eat, sleep, change my underwear regularly, and go to the toilet. I pay my bills and keep my appointments. I read magazines and watch TV. I somehow remember to file my income tax return, but somehow forget to send my dad a card for his birthday.

And through it all, throughout every insipid moment, thoughts of Linda. Linda, Linda—coursing through every waking minute; bounding from one dream to the next through every hour of sleep.

I drag my ass over to the university and spend hours hanging out in the English department office. I've never been so maniacally sociable in my life, eager to talk to anyone. Undergraduates, secretaries, janitors—anyone.

I throw myself into teaching; my classes have never been better. Anything that takes my mind off of this woman, if only for an hour, is like a painkilling drug—but one that quickly wears off, and with unpleasant side effects. Case in point: I hawk *Hamlet* to a roomful of politely inattentive freshmen, and try to turn them on to the lush cadence of Polonius' farewell speech to his son Laertes. My pride in this passage as I unfurl it for the class is almost like I wrote it myself. Fortunately for me though, my students are far too preoccupied with chomping on their hoagie sandwiches and slurping from their little styrofoam cups of coffee to notice that I've spent over a half hour absently saying "Laveccio" instead of "Laertes."

God damn her. Where the hell is she?

In another couple of days it will be exactly one month since the lady vanished. All things being equal, I will probably mark this red letter day—or night—by doing more or less what I'm doing right now: sitting alone in my apartment with a six pack of Miller High Life and a tubular canister of potato chips (more like potato 'things,' actually—stacked one on top of the other like my childhood collection of baseball cards), watching the "late, late" on TV.

Actually, this particular night has been a little different. At the moment, I am sitting here sort of shaking my head and talking to myself, having just come in an hour or so ago from a "date." That's right, a "*date.*" My first "date" with another woman in over a year.

I couldn't hold out. And neither could any of my friends or relatives, whom I have been slowly driving crazy.

"Man, just go out with someone," advised Lamarr Williams, my neighbor across the hall, evidently weary of listening to me pacing around the apartment and talking to my transistor radio at 2:00 a.m.

"Find someone else, hon'" suggested my landlady, who stopped by a couple of days ago to satisfy her curiosity over why I hadn't mailed her my rent checks for the months of March and April.

"*Shmuck*, stop moping around and get the hell off your butt," counselled my dad, who phoned here yesterday to express his displeasure at not receiving his customary birthday card.

"Go out and get laid," my best friend and colleague David Kaplan offered simply.

So, I called up an old friend, a woman my age, who started graduate school around the same time I did. An archeologist, no less. In charge of a warren of storerooms deep within the bowels of the University Museum. Another graduate student who'd fallen between the cracks. Another perennial, another "Fixture." We'd had a short but tempestuous "thing" together during our first year of grad school, ages and ages ago. I wondered if there might still be a warm "glowing ember" between us that we could rekindle.

"Oh shit," she groaned when I got her on the phone, "to what do I owe this all too rare pleasure?"

"I decided it's been too long since I've heard any real, first-rate, quality sarcasm. Hello Irene; what's new?", I intoned, somewhat sheepishly.

A weary sigh, and then, "*'WHAT'S NEW'*," she repeated, accenting each word and exhaling dramatically. "Well, let's see…" she paused again for effect. I was already starting to deeply regret this phone call. "A lot of Mayan pottery, some really cool obsidian jewelry from one of the burial sites at Tikal, a few more or less complete Mayan skeletons, another five pounds or so in my hips and ass, and a love-life so shitty and *empty* I wouldn't wish it on my worst enemy. What's new with *you*?"

"Oh…Well, you know," I began halfheartedly.

"Wait a minute, don't tell me…Poor Danny, did that disgustingly thin and hideously beautiful woman I've been seeing you around with finally get your number and dump you?"

"Well actually, she seems to have walked out on me, yeah." I replied, nodding my head against the receiver.

"Good for her! Beauty *and* brains, obviously. Remarkable display of intelligence from someone so attractive." Irene let out a long breathy sigh; her voice softening, she said, "Oh what the hell. I *know* I'm going to regret this—in fact, I'm pretty sure I regret it *already*—but why not stop by here around five'ish. We'll go somewhere for dinner, and you can tell me all the gory details."

Since the day I met her, a day in which Iran hostage crisis stories were still appearing on the second or third page of the *Philadelphia Inquirer* and disco music held almost total sway over the AM band of the radio, Irene has been not "pretty" really, but rather what is called a "handsome woman." Great bone structure. Clean, fresh good looks. Shoulder length auburn hair framing an honest, well-built face. A face that, back home in her native New Hampshire, would probably become marvelously windblown and craggy as she got older.

Another five or ten years, I mused as she greeted me in the museum's little front lobby, and she would start looking a little like the actress Colleen Dewhurst in her middle years. A woman could do a lot worse.

Emerging from the depths of the storage catacombs, Irene wore a somewhat dingy calve-length laboratory smock, its tent-like shapelessness accomplishing nothing toward hiding her still desirable, still provocative body. Like she had said over the phone, a little wider in the hips since the last time I saw her, but still that comfortably voluptuous figure that, in my first month of grad school, had made me feel suddenly a lot better about moving to Philadelphia.

I gave her an admiring once-over as she glided toward me. She gave *me* a mock scowl, followed by a hurried laugh and said, "Hang on for a sec—I'll be with you as soon as I ditch this sexy lab coat."

We climbed into her car—an ancient Volvo held together with chewing gum and spit—and wended our way downtown through the afternoon traffic. We hit a gridlock just over the South Street bridge and sat almost silently while Irene, clutching the wheel and jerking her head around, attempted to find some escape route out of the snarl.

The cars began moving again—probably right after some policeman up ahead decided to stop directing the traffic and to let it take its natural course. We sailed down into Center City and landed eventually at a small new French restaurant that Irene had heard about and was hot to try.

The place was indeed brand new, not yet a month old. Nevertheless, it followed the predictable pattern of the Philadelphia "restaurant renaissance." Small and cramped. Soft lights and lots of simply framed, kitschy art work on cream-white stucco walls. Soft, barely audible music—piano and flute, it always seems like—from a CD player on a shelf behind the wine bar. A jungle of ferns and hanging plants. A jumble of smart, very earnest looking young men and women observing the precise rituals of upscale dining. Flashing all the right looks and making all the right noises. Opening up and sharing candid bits of self-gossip over glasses of wine and very spare, very stingy little servings of food. Undercooked, fussily seasoned, and extravagantly overpriced food. Business as usual. Thank God for McDonald's.

A crisp looking young waitress in her mid twenties led us to a table and handed us menus like she was doing us a big favor. Irene, glad of an evening out and determined to enjoy herself, let it go by. A century or so later the waitress returned and took our orders, aloof and quite obviously bored. Irene and I relaxed and settled in.

It had obviously been some time since Irene was last out, at least out with a man. She talked as though she had just rediscovered her vocal cords and wanted to try them out to see if they still worked.

They did. Irene proceeded to update me on the course of her life since our last long talk. The expression she used, in fact—over and over again—was "trajectory." The "trajectory" of her life. The "trajectory" of her relationships. The "trajectory" of her thinking and personal development. *Oy.*

Actually, I knew I was in trouble quite early on when her lips parted and the phrase "self empowerment" came rolling out of her mouth and onto the table, soon to be joined there by similar droppings of gobbledygook. I stopped counting the number of times she used the word "perspectives" when she hit the magic number 10.

After a few minutes I was already starting to wonder whether Irene and I were participating in the same conversation. An hour or so and several glasses of wine later, and I was seriously wondering whether she was even there in the same room with me—or was I attempting to talk to a videotaped hologram being beamed at me from somewhere else.

By the time we had finished our coffee and signalled Miss Personality for our check, we were staring fixedly at our empty dessert dishes, with nothing much left to say. We drove back to West Philly, alternating between halfhearted attempts at small talk and bouts of pensive silence. Irene dropped me in front of my building; a quick chaste kiss, an exchange of polite goodbyes. By unspoken agreement, we seemed to have decided that there wasn't much point in trying for anything more.

And so, here I am. Sitting in front of the TV, tossing back cans of Miller's and practically inhaling a tube of these new wave potato chips (I am hungry as hell from that meager little meal).

And as I eat, I ponder. I glance over at the birthday card—still unmailed—that I finally got around to buying for my dad. I think of my parents, and their life and times: Boy met girl. They fell in love. World War II happened. Then the war was over and they got married, living happily ever after. Or if not "happily," than at least comfortably resigned. Something they were willing to "settle for."

I think of *me*, and my life and times. Just a few years back it seems, when I was in college, when I was a kid: Boy met girl. They fell in love. Or at least they hung out together, *making* love.

Did I miss something? Did something happen along the way that I was somehow too preoccupied to notice? When was it exactly that women became so utterly incomprehensible? At what precise point in time did this occur? Where was I when this was going on?

Goddamn it Linda, where are *you*?

She's back. Almost six weeks since our last crimson night together, Linda Laveccio is back. I don't know where she's been, let alone—for the moment—why she left. What really worries me is that I don't think I know *who* she has become. Has a stranger returned to me, wearing a clever Linda Laveccio disguise? I guess we'll get all this ironed out soon enough.

About all I have a handle on at the moment is the fact that she's returned, a fact gleaned—will wonders never cease?—from my mailbox at the English department. For anyone seeking a quiet, forgotten little corner of the world, completely off the beaten track and all but untouched by modern civilization, one need look no further than my mailbox. The Land that Time Forgot. So rarely disturbed by mail or messages it probably contains traces of eighteenth century Philadelphia dust. So completely irrelevant and out of the way, spymaster Jim Phelps could have safely picked up his tape recorded messages there from "The Secretary," in episodes of *Mission Impossible*.

Nevertheless, I meander into the office around 2:00 in the afternoon, glance lackadaisically into my mailbox—just for form's sake—and there it is. One of those little pink *"While-U-Were-Out"* slips, folded length-wise and thrust into my mailbox, looking almost as though it were astonished to be there. Nowhere near as astonished as *I* am though, as I gasp and yank the note out of the box. In the graceful, almost gothic handwriting of Ms. Vanessa Crawford—the English department's "Administrative Assistant" and yet another university Fixture—the note reads: *"Linda called. She says she's back."* Nothing more, except for a check-mark next to the line, *"Please Call."*

My heart beating like a kettle drum—I'm almost sure that Vanessa can hear it all the way across the office—I dial Linda's number. She answers the phone on what seems like the thousandth ring.

"Hello, Linda," I practically pant, "welcome back to the big city."

A quick chuckle from Linda, and then, "Yeah, right. The 'big city.' Hi, Danny, you got my message?" A pause. "How've you been?"

Something in Linda's voice sets off an alarm bell in my head. Anger? (But at *what*?) Defensiveness? Or worse—detachment? Whatever it is, it has put me on guard.

"Well...I guess I've been okay. Yeah, fine. So, Linda, tell me, where have you been?"

"Danny, I had a lot to think about. A lot to try and sort out."

"Jesus, Linda. You've been gone long enough to sort out everything from the Arab-Israeli conflict to our balance of trade problems with Japan. What the hell got into you?" I stop when I realize I'm starting to whine.

"Look, Danny, I don't need this kind of shit now, okay?"

We hold the phone in silence for a moment, stepping back from the edge, catching our breath. Upset as I may be, I have enough sense to know that the last thing I want—the last thing I could handle—would be for her to get pissed off and hang up.

I take a deep breath and say placatingly, "All right. How about if I come over, we have a cup of coffee? Or whatever?" My voice trails off lamely.

She takes so long to reply I think, with mounting dread, that she has hung up the phone after all. Finally I hear her sigh and say, "Later. Come by later, okay? We'll go out someplace for a quick supper and sort of take things from there."

We say our goodbyes and get off the phone. My moron heart beating so hard it hurts, I cannonball out of the office feeling better than I have felt in six long weeks. I can't imagine what I'm going to do to pass the time for the rest of this afternoon.

The woman that comes out of her apartment to open the glass entryway door looks like Linda—*my* Linda—and then again doesn't. Same olive complexion, same sparkling dark eyes. Same dimpled half-smile, same gliding walk. And yet, there have been changes. Some are immediately obvious while others are less apparent, but there. Definitely there.

The first thing I notice is the hair. The beautiful shimmering hair that cascaded down to the middle of her back has been cut to shoulder length. And something else—'permed,' do they call it? There is a curl and a TV-commercial body-'n-bounce to her hair that wasn't there before. Okay, no problem. I can live with it.

I guess I can live with the eye makeup also, the different style of earrings, and the jewelry. What I'm not sure I can live with—what is making me feel suddenly very uncomfortable—are the "vibes" being radiated by this brave new version of Linda Laveccio. As ecstatic as I am to see her, something feels wrong.

She looks at me for a moment, almost appraisingly, and then throws her arms around my neck. The lacerating kiss that follows is like an electroshock treatment, jolting away my sense of unease but leaving me vague and disoriented. She turns away with that gut-wrenching smile and leads me into the apartment.

We decide to cook and have dinner "in." Or rather Linda decides, and I agree. She has made preparations, it seems: ground beef, some sort of green colored pasta, salad vegetables, and a French bread are laid out on the blond wooden kitchen counter—like the parts for a Swiss watch being repaired by a master craftsman. A tangy smelling sauce simmers and bubbles in a pot on the stove. A red ceramic bottle of Almaden stands chilling in the fridge. God, how I've missed this woman.

Linda hands me a can of beer and a sharp cleaver, assigning me the task of making salad. We putter around the kitchen making small talk, getting comfortable with each other again. Avoiding the issues. Will we get to those issues later, I wonder?

Dinner is ready in the blink of an eye. The kitchen is hot on this early May evening; we set the table out in the living room. We maintain our reserve as we have our dinner, preferring to let the TV set in the corner do most of the talking, to be our alibi for companionable silence.

The evening takes the form of a short smooth road, with only one destination and no detours. Moments after the last dish has been washed, the last glass put away, we are in bed.

I attack this woman with an ardor born and nurtured through six weeks of unrequited longing. I inhale her like a diver too long under water, finally coming up for air.

Linda responds with a mixture of emotions I do not understand.

As physically passionate as ever, I suppose, but with something—irony? jadedness?—I have never seen in her before. At times I feel a sadness coming from her, seeming almost to evolve into anger, or resentment. Whatever it is though, I notice it only barely at the level of consciousness as I go through the night in a crimson haze.

Linda is already up and moving around the bedroom when I awaken shortly after dawn. A soft light glows from a green shaded desk lamp on the table near the window. Hearing me stir, she smiles, plants a kiss on my forehead and climbs back into bed next to me.

With mock seriousness, I survey my body for bite marks and bruises. Lovetaps; our old morning-after joke. Linda runs her hand across a sore spot on my neck, distractedly. And, again I think, with sadness.

Her mood makes me uncomfortable; I try to lighten things up. "Next time," I say, touching the tender spot on my neck, "I think I'll bring along a doctor, or at least a registered nurse."

Linda drops her hand from my neck and pulls away from me. She sits up, draws her legs up to her chest and wraps her arms around them. She rests her head on her knees and closes her eyes. I watch this nervously, enduring her silence.

"Danny," she murmurs finally, "there's not going to be a 'next time.' At least not with me."

Boom. There it is.

Before I can speak, she says, "How should I put this? I'm...involved, Danny...with someone else."

"What...*who*...?" My throat is so constricted I can barely breathe.

"It's someone I've known for a while. Someone I got to know a lot better during the last month or so."

"So that's what you've been doing all this time? Getting '*involved*'? Jesus Christ!" I know I'm about to 'lose it.'

"Danny..."

"Okay," I say, trying to regain control, "just tell me, who *is* this guy? How long have you known him? Where the hell does he live?"

Linda lifts her face away from her knees. She lets go of her legs, props a pillow against the wall and leans back against it. She sighs, a faint smile playing on her face.

"Well, as a matter of fact, it's someone I knew before I met you. From around my second year of college. She's a teacher now, and she lives in New York."

It takes a moment or two for this to sink in.

I jerk around sideways to look at her, really *seeing* her, perhaps for the first time. "'She'? Did you say '*she*'?"

Linda turns toward me, raises her eyebrows and slowly nods her head up and down. "Yeah," she says, her voice suddenly stronger, "*SHE*."

Philadelphia wears the month of May like a perky young girl in a brand new, bright showy dress. The midmorning warmth is gentle and soothing. Dappled sunlight dances on new green leaves and fresh blooming flowers. All around the campus everyone is outdoors, moving with a bounce, lustily imbibing the gorgeous spring day. Great looking young people are everywhere, hustling off to classes, walking arm in arm, tossing frisbees, luxuriating on the newly mowed grass.

I sit on a stone bench near the main thoroughfare of the campus, drinking black coffee from a styrofoam cup and watching the world parade by. A rich, beautiful pageant.

I feel strangely mellow, or is it merely the mellowness that comes with emotional exhaustion? We parted amicably, Linda and I. Just a couple of hours ago. We made each other promise to remain friends, and *I* at least intend to keep that promise. Hell, I even agreed to attend the "Commitment Ceremony" that Linda and her new lover are planning for late July in New York.

As I tilt my head back to down the last of the coffee, I see the buildings of the university rising up through the foliage all around me, lush and majestic in the morning sunlight. I greet them lovingly, with an almost filial devotion.

I look around, comforted and consoled, knowing with as much certainty as is possible in this uncertain world that I will be here for the rest of my life. Face it, I don't belong out there in the "real world." I'm just barely getting by *here*, in this ivy-covered "make believe" one.

Besides, in this small cozy little world I've come to know so well, there are always new possibilities, always new reasons for hope. I heard just last week from our department chairman that I'll be teaching another summer course, first summer session. Another Shakespeare course, for a whole new bunch of students.

I am already looking forward to the class as I sit here in the sun, surveying the passing scene. Who can say?—I just might meet someone interesting.

You never know.

Meditations

Home With Some Old Friends

I was recently reunited with some very close old friends. Around 2,000 of them, more or less, came over to my Ra'anana apartment last week, and they have permanently moved in. Okay, I'll explain.

Back in the closing days of 1979, I was a graduate student in anthropology at the University of Pennsylvania, waiting endlessly for my approval from the Indonesian government to do my doctoral fieldwork on one of their 13,000 islands. I had completed all of my coursework, passed all of my exams, had secured a sizable research grant, and needed only a nod from Jakarta—for which I was waiting, month after month after month. I had almost decided to give up waiting, abandon anthropology and join the circus when the long-awaited Indonesian entry visa came in the mail. To make matters even more exciting, the visa was timed to expire about two weeks after my receipt of it, so the accompanying letter, festooned with roughly 1,000 official stamps and signatures, advised me to decamp from Philadelphia as quickly as possible, haul my (then) young self over to Indonesia, and report to the Ministry of Immigration in Jakarta, forthwith.

With almost dervish-like abandon, I began to pack—up till 6:am for four nights in a row, packing everything I had, which consisted of around two thousand books and a few tobacco pipes. I developed astounding dexterity as that long first night wore on—fold the box, wet the packing tape, make the box, line the box with plastic, pack the box with books, seal the plastic, close the box, wet more packing tape, seal the box. Bingo, bango, bongo.

Everything that defined me at that time went into those boxes, including a couple of hundred books on Southeast Asia, a roughly equal number of volumes about American Indians, and an additional tome or two on virtually every ancient civilization from Tikal to Timbuktu. Not to mention the tobacco pipes.

What was I thinking, back in those dear, dead days as I hurriedly packed my life away? I thought I'd be coming back in a couple of years, to unpack those boxes and resume my life—as an anthropologist, an academic, an urbane pipe-smoking bon vivant, teaching in some fine university and taking my place among the ranks of young aspiring professionals. But life, as they say, is something that happens while you're planning something else.

Those two years in Indonesia were followed by thirteen more in the Philippines—other interests, other directions, numerous other careers, a wife, two children, and a whole different life. What's more, I eventually stumbled upon a small but vibrant Jewish community in Manila, which led to a reawakening of my Jewish identity and our *aliyah* to Israel four years ago.

And the boxes of books? Well, while I wandered, so did they. First to a barn in East Bridgewater, Massachusetts. Then to an attic in Quincy, a warehouse in Hingham, and finally to a U-Store-It facility in Weymouth, MA.—all thanks to the careful ministrations of my poor, long-suffering parents. For some 22 years, through my adventures in Indonesia, my lengthy sojourn in the Philippines, and my final homecoming to Israel, the boxes—and everything in them—rested peacefully in the dark.

Until now.

Deciding it is time to close some of the innumerable open circles in my life—and resolving that Israel is indeed my final home, I sent for the boxes. They arrived last week—56 to be exact, borne on the shoulders of three somewhat exhausted looking moving men, who breathlessly asked if I was planning to open a bookstore as they piled them floor to ceiling in my living room. My wife and children stood huddled in a corner, contemplating the rising pyramid of boxes, as I rushed out to buy some new bookcases—a lot of new bookcases.

Now, one week later, I sit blissfully surrounded by some 2,000 books—crammed cheek-to-jowl in my small Ra'anana apartment. Like a time capsule unearthed and reopened, they reconnect me to another time in my life, to an earlier version of me.

My wife wanders bemusedly around the flat, mumbling her doubts about the practical applications of *Political Systems of Highland Burma*. My son—a serious yeshiva student—finds little of interest in *Navaho Witchcraft*. My ten year-old daughter, bless her soul, sits cross-legged on the floor in her B'nei Akiva uniform, gamely surveying *Structure and Function in Primitive Society*.

Acquaintances in Ra'anana wonder where I've been lately. I'm home with some old friends—minus the tobacco pipes, which my wife pitched into the trash.

The Trouble with Hebrew

It happened again today. I climbed aboard a battered, soot-encrusted No.46 bus, which never fails to remind me of the *African Queen* as it wends its way, groaning and wheezing, down Yefet Street through darkest Jaffa. The driver, recognizing me from many previous expeditions, made a face that could pass for a smile and said to me, "Blah, blah, blah! Blah, blah-blah-blah-blah, blah-blah. Blah, blah-blah, blah?"

All right, he didn't really say that. That was what I heard. What he actually said was, "Good morning! I haven't seen you for a while. Have you been feeling all right?" Unfortunately, he said it in Hebrew.

I did what I normally do in these situations. I smiled stupidly, nodded my head up and down like a slack-jawed yokel, and made a few random noises in response that included a few words of the Philippine tribal language I spoke years ago as a Peace Corps volunteer. I handed my interlocutor five shekels, grabbed my ticket and change, and lummoxed toward a seat at the back of the bus. As we snaked our way through almost unmoving Jaffa traffic, I mentally made yet another withdrawal from my account at the Bank of Self-Esteem.

I did not make *aliyah* to Israel last week. It wasn't last month either, or even last year. I have in fact lived, worked, laughed and cried in this country for almost 5 years. And my inability to communicate in Hebrew—beyond a few primitive gestures and grunts—has been a source of almost unutterable embarrassment.

In other periods of my life, I have been variously fluent in Indonesian, functional in Filipino, and fluent again in an ethnic language of a remote Philippine island. But after some seven months of *ulpan* and almost five years in Israel, I still come across like one of the cave-man characters in the movie *Quest for Fire* whenever I try to speak Hebrew.

The reason for this has eluded me—until now. A couple of weeks ago, I received a delightful e-mail message from an dear old friend from graduate school—always supportive, never judgmental—who helpfully offered her astute analysis of my problem with Hebrew. "Is this merely your usual sloth," she asked, "or have you also become a total moron?"

As I e-mailed her a couple of computer-killing viruses in reply, I began to seriously reflect on why I have not been able to acquire even the rudiments of Hebrew after almost five long years of careful study and effort. After a few moments of intensive contemplation—interspersed, of course, with a trip to the bathroom, a somewhat testy phone call from my landlady, another glance at the *Jerusalem Post's* sports page, a telephoned order for one large pizza with extra cheese, a follow-up call 45 minutes later to demand to know when the pizza was coming, a late dinner and an episode of the *Sopranos*—I stumbled upon the answer: My brain is full.

Now the experts—neuologists, neurophysiologists, educational psychologists, and others of that ilk—tell us that the human brain is an instrument of almost unfathomable complexity, capable of storing, retrieving and analyzing a virtually infinite amount of information. Experience, however, tells us that the human brain is a lot like a 3.5 inch computer diskette—or, more accurately, one of those old 5 inch low-density floppy disks—which can absorb only so many bytes of data before it sends you a message reading: "Destination drive full."

So, what do you do when one of your computer diskettes is virtually chock-a-block full of files, as tightly packed as a Jamaican cigar? Well, if you're anything like me, you probably entomb the diskette into a diskette storage case—wedged between, say, a diskette containing your unfinished novel and another with an old game called *Leather Goddesses of Phobos*—or you simply decide to delete one or two superfluous, unnecessary files.

Imagine, for just a moment, how wonderful it would be to delete some of the 'superfluous, unnecessary' files stored in your cerebral cortex, or lodged far back in your *medulla oblongata*. I know, with nary a second thought, what I would hasten to get rid of. I'd zap Rudyard Kipling's *Gunga Din* for starters, memorized under extreme duress from an anglophile English teacher in the eighth grade, who considered the poem to be part of the "romance of colonialism." Next to go would be Polonius' farewell speech to Laertes, *Hamlet*; Act I, Scene III, which I was brutally forced to commit to memory in grade nine.

As the song goes, "we've only just begun." Having deleted a few more poems, plays, parables and inspirational speeches branded onto my brain by the Boston public school system, I would gladly eliminate such treasures as the words to every Top 40 song from 1958 to 1979, the plot-lines and dialogue from every episode of the *Twilight Zone*, 45 years of TV advertisement jingles, the complete roster of the 1962 Boston Red Sox, the opening theme songs of such TV shows as *The Pruitts of Southampton* and *My Mother the Car*, the secret rhyme recited by comic-book hero Green Lantern when he slipped on his magic ring, the complete roll call of my 10th grade gym class, the names of children I went to nursery school with, the combination to my mail box in college, and every telephone number I have ever had.

Then, maybe, I would have some room in my head for Hebrew.

I am afraid, however, that dreams must remain dreams. Until someone, somewhere, comes up with a way for me to jettison about cerebral 2 gigabytes of worthless information, I will simply have to make do. The next time my friend on the No. 46 bus—or any other monolingual speaker of Hebrew—feels like having a *schmooze*, I will stand up straight, hold my head high, and recite Kipling's *Gunga Din*.

A Note From School

The note, scrawled in pencil on a frayed sheet of white lined composition paper, had obviously been written with an angry hand. The handwriting was a storm of deep black grooves and gauges, with a small gash where the pencil had torn through the paper. The message read, "Hello Parent. Rachel needs to tell you what happened in class today. Please sign this letter after she has told you what she did and have her return it to me tomorrow." Below that rather cryptic message were the scribbled initials of my daughter's teacher, and below that was a penciled line over which I was evidently supposed to sign my name.

I put the note down with a world-weary sigh and glanced up at my 11 year-old daughter, seated opposite me at the other end of the dining room table. Fortifying myself with a couple of deep breaths, I looked up at her expectantly over the top of my eyeglasses, my eyebrows slightly raised, and waited for her to speak. Whereupon my little princess—light of my life, apple of my eye, and comfort in my declining years—smiled sweetly and said, "A boy in my class was bothering me. I told him to leave me alone, but he wouldn't. So I ripped the hood off his jacket, took it to the bathroom, and threatened to flush it down the toilet. He stopped bothering me after that." She accompanied this anecdote with a flutter of her eyelashes and a backhand flip of her wrist, as if to suggest that the matter was one of no great importance.

After staring at my daughter for several seconds with frank amazement, my mouth opened so wide I had to reach up and close it by hand, I came to my senses and assumed the role of irate father. Arranging my face into what I hoped was a suitably severe scowl, I launched into the obligatory Judge Hardy lecture on discipline, self-control, and learning to resolve problems calmly and rationally. As my colloquy on stoicism droned tediously on, reinforced with references ranging liberally from the *Ethics of the Fathers* to the *Analects of Confucius*, I thought to myself "Wow! Good for her!" and realized that I would never, *ever*, have had the chutzpah to do anything like that at her age—or, truth be told, even now.

Since making aliyah from the Philippines almost five years ago, not a day has passed without at least one moment in which I have gazed meditatively at my wife and two children—three happy, purposeful, well-adjusted individuals chatting animatedly around the dinner table—and asked myself, "Who *are* these people, and where is the family I brought here?" What happened to the three rather shy, introverted people that accompanied me on that exhausting voyage from Manila, and who wandered with me, silent and overwhelmed, up and down Ahuza Street in our first days in Ra'anana?

In a word, what happened to them was *Israel*.

The decision to come here was not an easy one. My children knew no home other than the Philippines, where they were born and raised as I lurched through a succession of U.S. government jobs. Their early life was comfortably crowded with maids and nannies attending to their every whim and need. As a result, neither of my children ever fell down while learning to walk, or at any time after that; numerous pairs of hands were always there to catch them before they hit the ground.

I knew that wrenching my children away from the gentle comforts of growing up in the Philippines would be difficult enough; even harder to deal with was the realization that neither of them was likely to receive in Israel the broad, renaissance education I had acquired, however unwillingly, growing up in Boston a generation or two ago. Neither would ever read Herman Melville or James Joyce, thrill to either the Boston Symphony or B.B. King, see the Unicorn Tapestries or an walk through an exhibit of Japanese *netsuke*, or even learn to how mix an acceptable martini. My son would likely never experience the poignant, character-building sorrow of watching the Red Sox blow an easy World Series win in the last pitch of the last inning of the second-to-last game; my daughter would never know the joys of a Boston Pops concert by the Charles River on a fragrant summer night.

And yet, as I began to stumble upon more and more Israelis in Manila before making aliyah—business people, backpackers, Embassy officials and so on—I was struck by the somewhat surprising observation that they all seemed fairly well put-together mentally. They were, to a man (and woman), relatively confident, relaxed, self-possessed, straightforward types, with no outward evidence of anything unduly complicated going on in their minds. They seemed, well…happy. So, although mindful of the dangers of "sampling error," I looked at these Israeli expatriates in the Philippines and decided that I could do far worse for my children than to bring them to Israel and make them Israelis.

Today, some five years later, the results of this decision fill my days with quiet satisfaction and never-ending wonder: two rugged, self-assured, self-reliant, well-adapted children who, for better *and* worse, act like they were born here.

As I glanced down at the note and searched my pockets for a pen, I reflected that my little Israeli daughter would probably never be induced to read anything by Moliere, Margaret Mead, or Yukio Mishima. She is, however, learning to respect and take care of herself as she grows up in an increasingly difficult world.

I scratched my initials over the pencilled line drawn in anger by my daughter's teacher, with just the faintest trace of a smile on my face that I simply could no longer suppress. I hoped my daughter didn't notice it as I handed her back the note.

He and She

He, not a day less than 90 years old, sits quietly in his wheel-chair, his pale bald head covered with what must be the last Panama hat in all of Israel. She, probably not a day more than 30, sits next to him at the edge of a bench, gently patting his arm and nodding her head occasionally when he speaks. His lined face and bright gray eyes sparkle with recollections of youthful years in a small town on the marshy banks of a tea-colored river called the Pripyat. Her dark brown eyes smile with visions of verdant sun-dappled mountains tumbling downward toward white-sand beaches and a shimmering blue tropical sea.

He, born long ago in Poland, likes to sit in this same spot every day, watching the life of this bustling Israeli city pulse and parade colorfully by him. She, his Filipina care-giver, wheels him here every afternoon, sits softly by his side and dreams her dreams of home.

His speech is a cholent of Hebrew and English, heavily seasoned with Yiddish. Her "English" it turns out, is mostly Tagalog, resonating with the lilting, musical cadences of southern Luzon. And yet at some level, beyond language or perhaps somewhere deep beneath it, they seem to understand each other perfectly.

He tells her about long-ago weddings and radiant Sabbaths, of *Purimspiels* and Passover seders—a thousand shtetl *simchas* from decades ago. She tells him about joyful town fiestas, colorful processions of saints, *Flores de Mayo* parades and pious *Noche Buena* feasts. Hour after hour, day after day; they have learned to find familiar landmarks in their visits to each other's pasts.

They arrive at their usual spot this day as everyday—a bone-thin, frail old man and a short, almost boyish-looking young woman, each happy to escape the confines of a dark cluttered flat at the end of a row of three-story white apartment buildings on a somber Herzelia street. She glances at her watch and reaches for a small plastic bottle of mineral water from a basket by her feet.

"*Saba*," she says in her child-like voice, "it's time to take your medicine," as she hands him the bottle and four little pills of different shapes and colors. He rouses himself from a daydream, swallows the pills slowly, one by one. She moves to adjust his jacket collar; he stops her with a languid wave of his hand. They settle in and get comfortable, ready for the hours to roll by.

Once, there was a family. He had a wife—happily married for 48 years—and two daughters who grew up joyously smothering him with their love. The years marched happily on. But the wife died almost ten years ago after a lingering illness, and the daughters have long since married and moved away—both overseas, far away.

Once, there was a family. She had her parents, and five older brothers. They all stood with her, bright-eyed and smiling, on that golden day seven years ago as she, proudly bedecked in her crimson cap and gown, received her diploma and a bachelor's degree in education from a poor but prestigious teachers' college in Manila. It was not long after that, however, that those same smiling parents and five under-employed older brothers informed her that their continued survival required more money than she could provide with her meager teacher's salary. So, away she went, to a far-away, strife-torn country she knew only as the "Holy Land," to take care of a lonely old Jewish man.

Late morning slides into early afternoon. The sun becomes strong, and she rises from her perch at the edge of the bench to move his wheelchair slightly backward, into a bit of shade. He raises his hand in faint protest, but she gently moves him anyway, reminding him of the dangers of too much sun. He sighs and says he is hungry, so she reaches into the basket for the cheese sandwiches she made before leaving the old man's apartment. As they begin to eat, a No. 29 Egged bus slows down as it approaches them, the driver beeping his horn inquiringly. She waves the bus away; they are not going anywhere.

This afternoon, it seems, is a time for talk. His face darkens as his mind wanders inexorably back to a nightmare time and place. He tells her again, in words she does not understand but with emotion she can feel as intensely as he, of brutal violence and unspeakable horror—of shouting German soldiers and snarling dogs, of frightened women and silent men; of hiding in the cellar of a Polish family's house while parents and neighbors, brothers and sisters, cousins and friends, Rabbis and teachers, classmates and playmates are herded toward the edge of town, never to return, never to be seen again.

She tells him again, in words he does not understand but with emotion he can feel as intensely as she, some of the stories she grew up with—of a terrifying defeat and crushing surrender, of shouting Japanese soldiers and razor-sharp bayonets; of a grandfather, father and uncles herded down the sun-scorched, dusty roads of Bataan alongside the captured American troops, prodded and beaten for days without food or water, and dumped into a squalid prison camp to begin more than two years of starvation and torment.

Shadows lengthen as the afternoon wanes. They sit together, now in silence, their thoughts far away. The sun slowly departs, leaving a chill in the air—a chill felt acutely by a frail old man nearing the end of his days, and a care-giving young lady from a distant land of endless summer.

She rises from the bench and gathers their things. He returns to the present and angles his head forward expectantly as she unlocks the wheelchair and gently turns it in the direction of home. They amble forward together slowly, this day as every day, toward a dark cluttered flat at the end of a row of three-story white apartment buildings on a somber Herzelia street.

Don't Worry Israel, Nothing is Forever

"I just can't stand it anymore," she said to me as she lit another cigarette—her third in less than a half-hour. Her hand trembling as she spooned three heaping teaspoons of sugar into her coffee, she said, "Let's face it, the violence is never going to end. The Palestinians will never accept a Jewish state here, and they will never give up on terror. So that's why we're packing up and moving back to Baltimore."

"You can't be serious," I said, with genuine shock. "You and your husband are two of the most gung-ho, over-the-top Zionists I know. You *cannot* be serious."

"I'm deadly serious. We have five kids, and we're not prepared to raise them in an atmosphere of perpetual violence. There's just no end to it; it's going to go on forever."

Her words echoed in my brain this morning over breakfast, as I watched the news on CNN. One of their correspondents was wandering up and down Ben Yehuda Street in Jerusalem, collecting quotes to support his contention that Israelis have become "resigned to terror" and have come to see the possibility of being murdered as simply "a fact of life." The segment closed with one young man gazing dolefully into the camera and saying, "The violence will never end. This is forever."

Perhaps. Perhaps not.

I used to work in a refugee camp. Perched on a ridge amidst the jagged mountains of western Luzon, the sprawling Philippine Refugee Processing Center housed and cared for some 25,000 Southeast Asian "boat people"—Vietnamese, Cambodians and Laotians—prior to their eventual resettlement in the United States.

Each and every one of these people had some sort of dreadful story to tell. Many of the Vietnamese had spent years in labor camps or "re-education" camps, run by vengeful North Vietnamese army officers; virtually all of the Cambodians had endured three years of horror under Pol Pot and the Khmer Rouge. Yet despite their refugee status and the often very unhappy circumstances of their lives at that point, the Philippine government tried its best to make these people feel comfortable and "at home" during their temporary stay in the Philippines. The refugee camp thus had the look and feel of a small rural town, complete with a post office, a hospital, a public library with two neighborhood branches, schools, playgrounds, markets, gardens, shady arbors and, of course, Buddhist temples—lots of Buddhist temples, replete with saffron-robed, shaven-headed, refugee priests and monks.

At the end of a garden path in one of the camp's Vietnamese neighborhoods, there was a little grotto—shaded by coconut palm trees and emblazoned with bright, fragrant bougainvillea flowers—that overlooked a magnificent vista of the mountains beyond and the valley below. At the center of the grotto stood a painted cement statue of Kwan-yin, Mahayana Buddhism's Goddess of Mercy. Beneath her feet and supporting the statue was a cement pedestal fashioned to look like a giant lotus blossom. Around the lotus blossom was a low painted-cement wall, on which was inscribed a brief message, in Vietnamese, Khmer, Lao and English. The message, inscribed by some forgotten sculptor to the camp's refugees, read: "Don't worry. This will pass. Everything does."

From long ago and far away, these words have come back to me a lot lately, resonating softly in my mind throughout the past 21 months of terror and bloodshed here in Israel. I hear these words, in an almost subliminal whisper, every time someone tells me there's no hope, that there will we no end to our present suffering, or that the violence and murder will continue forever. The message repeats itself with particular insistence whenever I hear someone talk about leaving.

Most of us, I think, have a tendency to believe that the way things are at present is the way they are likely to be forever. And yet, we have all witnessed enough stunning reversals of fortune in recent years—some of them almost epic—to remind us that nothing lasts forever. Many of us can recall a time, for example, in which it seemed that the war in Vietnam would continue to rage forever, without end, without hope, and with our children's children either perennially protesting the war or flushing Vietcong guerillas out of the Mekong Delta. Eventually though, the war—fought initially against the Japanese, then the French, then the U.S., and finally against a South Vietnamese army of toy soldiers, came to an end.

It also was not so long ago that the Soviet Union seemed invincible, standing mightily astride the world, with Leonid Brezhnev's Red Army invading Afghanistan while Jimmy Carter's Foreign Service Officers were being held hostage in Iran. Who could have imagined then that the USSR would simply dry up and blow away a mere decade later—beaten, in the words of the comic strip *Doonesbury*, by expensive American high-tech, cheap wheat, and good old rock and roll?

Who would have dreamt, in the *early* 1990's, when it seemed that the U.S. could do nothing right and Japan could do nothing wrong, that in the *late* 1990's the Japanese economy would crumble while America's economy soared? And what about 'that other' unsolvable conflict—our "sister" quagmire in Northern Ireland. Did any of us ever expect to see Catholics and Protestants begin to come to terms, or hear the IRA declare that they were putting their weapons "beyond use?"

Nothing is forever.

Granted, the war for survival that we are fighting here in Israel is probably far from over. Perhaps inevitably, we're in for more violence. Almost certainly, things are going to get worse before they get better.

And yet, in the aftermath of each new outbreak of violence against Israelis—even as I watch the heart-rending scenes on TV—I cannot forget the words that once adorned a painted cement statue of the Goddess Kwan-yin. "Don't worry. This will pass. Everything does."

An Accidental Israeli

Congratulate me.

I have just reached an important milestone in life: five years in Israel. I realize, of course, that this short span of time pales before those reached by people who have lived in this country for decades—who built houses amidst sand dunes, who ventured out to establish communities in the middle of vast orange orchards, and who fondly remember their now-bustling cities back when they were miniscule *moshavim*, lacking traffic lights or even paved roads.

My unique milestone draws its significance not from the *amount* of time I have spent here, but rather from the sheer *irony* of my being here at all. I hold the distinction of being perhaps the least likely human being on this planet to have made aliyah. Five years in Israel is no mean feat for a guy who spent most of his life swearing that he would never, *ever*, set foot here.

I was Bar Mitzvah'ed almost 40 years ago in a Conservative synagogue on the outskirts of Boston, where my famously non-religious parents piously attended services for an hour or two every Yom Kippur. That Bar Mitzvah, attended by my large family of Kennedy-style super-liberals, proved to be my last brush with Judaism, in any shape or form, for more than three decades.

I walked out of the synagogue and into the 1960's. Following a rather colorful Flower Child adolescence, about which the less said the better, I went on to college—in New York's Greenwich Village—where I majored in anthropology and 'minored' in East Asian studies. My subsequent graduate school years saw me in Indonesia, doing my doctoral fieldwork on the island of Borneo, where the only Jewish face I saw in two years was my own reflection in the turbid, slow-moving water of jungle rivers and streams.

Those two years in Indonesia were followed by thirteen in the Philippines, where I lived with a hill tribe in a remote mountain village for three years, lived and worked among Indochinese boat people in a refugee camp for six years, and then hopped around the country's 3,500 islands teaching and consulting for a year or two after that. I met, chased and eventually married a hard-working provincial social worker, had two beautiful children, and quickly learned to enjoy the life of an "ex-pat" American in the lush Philippine country-side. Judaism was, at best, a distant and irrelevant memory.

Then, when I least expected it, life's Great Referee flashed me a yellow card. An unexpected job offer with the Philippine government's Department of Education brought us out of the boondocks and into Manila, where I soon heard faint but persistent rumors of the existence of a small but viable Jewish community. Intrigued by the image of Jews in the Philippines, I set out one Saturday to find them.

After I had wandered around Manila's business district for more than an hour, a small, squat, gray building adorned with a large iron menorah and topped with a golden dome loomed sharply into view. Cleverly camouflaged amidst the gleaming office towers and five-star hotels, set behind a tall wrought-iron gate and protected by uniformed Filipino security guards, the Philippines' one and only synagogue stood shockingly before me. Passing the rather elaborate security check, I entered the amazing little building to find an orthodox congregation of roughly 80 people, devoutly praying the morning service for Sabbath. Later, at the lavishly catered kiddush, a pale, bespectacled and very young man in a black velvet kippa introduced himself to me as the Rabbi (The Rabbi!!, I gawked. In the middle of Manila!!) and asked if this was my first visit to the shul.

"It's my first visit to *any* shul in more than thirty years," I said to him. He smiled, shook my hand, and said, "Welcome home."

Now, those of you who misspent your 1950's childhoods reading comic books will no doubt recall that Superman had a weekend getaway place at the North Pole, which he fondly referred to as his "Fortress of Solitude." Hidden and buried amidst the windswept snow and ice, the Fortress was filled with a myriad number of souvenirs, trophies, mementos and assorted brick-a-brack gathered from years of fighting crime in Metropolis, safeguarding America, and patrolling the immediate galaxy.

Still with me? Among Superman's favorite *tchochkes* at the Fortress was the Bottled City of Kandor—an actual, living city from his home planet Krypton, shrunk, somehow, to miniature size and housed in a small climate-controlled glass jar, which Superman kept on a lovely walnut Queen Anne side-table at the end of an upstairs hall. When Superman felt that he needed to be with his fellow Kryptonians, speak a little Kryptonese, eat a bit of *heimische* Kryptonite food and just generally reconnect with his Krypton roots, he would enter the Bottled City. Emerging from this sentimental journey a few hours later, a refreshed, recharged and re-motivated Superman would leave the North Pole and fly back to Metropolis, back to his never-ending battle for truth, justice, and the American Way—and his somewhat complicated relationship with Lois Lane.

Well, the little synagogue in Manila—nestled amongst the towering office buildings and five-star hotels of the city's business district—became *my* Bottled City of Kandor, a weekly haven from the stress of life and work, and a revitalizing return to my roots. I went every Saturday morning, to surround myself with Jewish faces, recharge my mind with Jewish conversation, and stuff myself with Jewish food.

But the trouble with having a bottled city, as Superman no doubt discovered after he finally broke down and married Lois Lane, is that sooner or later your wife wants to go into the bottle with you. After several weeks of wondering where I was sneaking off to every Saturday morning, my non-practicing-Catholic Filipina wife decided to accompany me to shul.

You can imagine, of course, what happened next: as it has so many times before, in places scattered throughout the world, the synagogue cast its irresistible spell. My wife found a seat in the women's section, and I spent the next couple of hours discreetly watching her watch Judaism as it unfolded before her. I watched as she opened a prayer book and slowly became engrossed in portions of the English translation. I saw her eyes widen as the ark was opened and a huge ornate Sephardi-style Torah, with gleaming polished silver crowns, was paraded around the sanctuary and taken up to the bimah. I caught her faint smile as the congregation began to sing. And later at the kiddush I noted, with little surprise, her evident fondness for kugel and chopped herring.

As we walked home I said, "Well, that's what I've been doing every Saturday. No big deal, right?" To which she replied, "Next week, we'll bring the kids."

Bring them we did—the next week, and every week thereafter. It soon became apparent to me that we were well on our way down a long new road I had never expected to travel. Regular synagogue attendance, involvement in the Jewish community, the beginnings of Sabbath observance, some tentative stabs at keeping kosher, weekly study sessions with the Rabbi, Hebrew lessons for the children—a gaudy kaleidoscope of Judaism flashed around us at dizzying speed and soon enveloped us completely.

When, after a year or so of this, my wife announced that she wanted to formally convert and raise our children in an authentically Jewish environment, I knew that it was time to leave the Philippines and make aliyah to Israel. My relatives in the U.S. simply sighed, shrugged, and pronounced this as fresh evidence of the sort of bizarre behavior they have always expected of me.

As no one from the Philippines had made aliyah since the end of World War II, a helpful young first secretary at the Israeli Embassy in Manila appointed himself as our *sheliach*, faxing Jerusalem almost daily with questions about how to do the paperwork. The Ambassador summoned us to his office, to satisfy himself that we were, as he put it, "for real." A stamp for our immigrant visas had to be sent by diplomatic pouch from the Israeli Embassy in India, as no such stamp was to be found any farther east then New Delhi. After more a year of planning, processing and paperwork, we were on our way.

We arrived at Ben Gurion Airport, dazed but excited, a little more than five years ago. In due course my wife was converted, the children studied and flourished in religious schools, and we slowly but inexorably became "Israelis."

Life, I have learned, is something that goes on while you are planning something else. Or, as my grandmother used to say, "Man plans, God laughs."

A Midwinter Night's Dream

Before anything else, I was conscious of suddenly being almost completely enveloped in a dark shadow. I glanced up from my copy of the *New Republic*, sent to me faithfully every week by my parents back in Boston. The man loomed over me—six feet tall at the very least, easily 250 pounds—an icon of eccentricity in a battered fedora, a long grey pony tail and an immense drooping mustache. "Excuse me," he rasped, extending a hand that looked big enough for me to sit in, "is this seat next to you taken?" It was not, and I noted with silent annoyance that neither were any of the other seats farther away from me.

At around 11:00 at night, the Central Bus Station in Tel Aviv becomes home to the inhabitants of another Israel, an Israel that few American Jews back in New York or Los Angeles would ever suspect exists. Dark, rumpled old men, wandering around the terminal selling ladies' cosmetics out of heavy bags strapped to their drooping shoulders. Ancient old ladies, their heads in faded scarves, schlepping from one bus platform to the next, their gnarled hands outstretched for a charitable shekel. Tough looking girls, their jaws moving violently around snapping wads of chewing gum, tight pants with bare midriffs, and spiky hair dyed in iridescent colors. Boyfriends of the tough girls—wiry guys sparkling with earrings and hair gel, noisy with coarse swagger. Gaggles of be-robed Ethiopians, dreamy haredim, sleeping soldiers, and half-crazed vendors loudly selling everything from ear-splitting rap music CDs to mounds of inedible looking coffee cake. A vibrant, garish carnival, now rendered even more colorful by the big man sitting next to me.

Anyone who rides the buses at night knows the type of guy this was: reasonably bright, not unpleasant, but with one screw in his head that someone forgot to tighten, one little wire that someone forgot to connect. I wonder why these people are drawn to me.

We started to talk, or rather *he* did as I put away my magazine, resigned to being his audience until the bus came. His accent was unmistakably New York, but everything else about him suggested a long stint of residence in Israel. He began to tell me the story of his life, year by year. Just as he got to 1956, a new year dawning pregnant with hope and promise, a big green 501 Egged bus pulled into the platform and started to take on passengers for Herzelia and Raanana. I climbed aboard and took my usual seat in front of the rear door. I suppose I wasn't really surprised as I was promptly joined by my new found 'friend,' who dropped heavily into the seat next to me. He patted my knee companionably as he continued his autobiography, bringing us now into 1957.

The man droned on as I drifted in and out, alternately paying bare attention and quietly starting to doze. Moments later, I found myself in a bizarre dream in which the man, still sitting next to me, was telling me loudly that he had a surefire way to end the Israeli-Palestinian conflict "once and for all." I shook myself awake and discovered that my big seat mate was, in fact, proclaiming that he had a surefire way to end the Israeli-Palestinian conflict, once and for all.

I would guess that after more than two years of our troubles with the Palestinians, each of us has heard and considered virtually every conceivable idea to end the bloodshed and achieve some sort of peace. Certain that I was about hear one or another of the usual proposals, I glanced at his long pony tail and said, "Wait. Don't tell me. We should re-start the Oslo process and return to the negotiating table."

"Yeah, right," he chortled. "A fat load of good that's accomplished."

"Okay," I said, somewhat chastened at having profiled him incorrectly, "Let's climb into our tanks, head on over to the West Bank, and pulverize them into submission. He shook his head slightly, gestured eastward and said, "Be my guest, friend, go 'pulverize' to your heart's content. But all that pulverizing hasn't accomplished a whole lot either, has it?"

"Transfer," I said, my voice rising. "You want to transfer the Palestinians to Jordan, right?"

"Wrong," he laughed. "Get real, *bubeleh*. We'd never get away with it. We toss so much as one Palestinian across the Jordan River and the whole world would be at our throats. Even the evangelical Christians would stop talking to us."

"So okay," I said, spreading my hands. "What have you got?"

He reached into an inside pocket of his tweed jacket and fished out two pairs of what appeared to be cheap sunglasses, each pair encased in shrink-wrapped cellophane. "These are the prototypes," he said as he tore open the cellophane. "I'm looking for financing to go into full production."

I glanced around nervously, searching for somewhere else to sit, as he held the glasses up for me to look at. On closer inspection, I could see that one pair, with blue plastic frames, had the left lens tinted red and the right lens tinted green. The other pair, with orange frames, had the left lens tinted green this time, and the right lens tinted red.

"Why, they're '3-D' glasses," I chortled urbanely, "kind of like the ones they used to give out in horror movies when I was a little kid. What are you going to do, take everyone in Israel to see *The House of Thirteen Ghosts*?"

My lunatic friend smiled and nodded approvingly, obviously appreciating the reference to a classically kitschy movie. He then glanced around the bus, pointing to a young Arab woman and her small daughter sitting in the first row. Handing me the glasses with the blue frames, he said, "Put these on. Keep your eyes focused on that lady and her little girl."

I put the glasses on and gasped as the woman and her daughter vanished into thin air. Everyone else on the bus was still there, right where they were before I put the glasses on. But the Arab woman and her daughter were gone. I yanked the glasses off, and lo and behold, they were back, right where they were before.

"Now you see them...", he said as I held the glasses out in front of me, "Now you don't!" he said as I slipped them back on.

"What...how...what the hell *are* these?" I yelled. He grabbed the glasses away from me and said, "They're my plan to bring the Israeli-Palestinian conflict to an end, once and for all. Magic eyeglasses—not three-dimensional, more like one-dimensional, since they let you see only one kind of people. The ones with the blue frames are for Jews. You put them on, and Arabs become invisible. The orange ones are for Arabs. They blot out any vision of Jews. I plan to mass produce these glasses and issue a blue pair to every Jew between the Jordan River and the Mediterranean, and an orange pair to every Arab."

I stared at him stupidly and said, "I don't get it."

Losing his patience with me, he replied, "Don't you see? The Arabs put on their orange glasses and think they're in a Palestine with no Jews! The Jews meanwhile slip on their blue glasses and presto!—a nice big Israel with no Arabs! Everybody's happy. End of story."

"End of story, until Jews and Arabs start blindly bumping into each other—especially in Jerusalem," I noted. My lunatic's face took on a hurt expression as he said," Well, I suppose you can find something wrong with any great idea if you try hard enough."

We rode the rest of the way in silence. As the bus turned onto Ahuza Street in Raanana, I shrugged and said, "Listen, those glasses are clever, I'll give you that. But using them to settle our problems with the Palestinians has got to be the craziest damn idea I've ever heard."

He let out a long, breathy sigh and said, "*Tateleh*, look at me." I looked at him. "Look me right in the eye and tell me some other idea. ANYTHING! Can you think of anything else to get us out of this mess?"

Well, it's now about one month after that fateful encounter. And although it did take me a few days to get used to them, these new eyeglasses are very, very comfortable.

Mr. Weissbord and Me

My militantly non-religious parents sent me to Hebrew School when I was a kid. Five days a week, an hour and a half a day. It was called the "Dorchester-Mattapan Hebrew School," and it was basically a warren of pokey little classrooms grafted on to the side and back of Temple Beth Hillel, on Morton Street in Boston. Believe it or not, I kind of enjoyed it, sort of.

Let me begin by saying first of all what it was *not*. It was not some kind of ultra-Orthodox *cheder* where we all sat around in little black hats and side curls. Nor was it some sort of desperately meaningful, obsessively relevant, earnestly Reform "Celebration of Jewish Experience." The 'Dor-Mat' Hebrew School was in fact an old style Conservative Hebrew School in the heart of an old style, working class, urban Jewish neighborhood in Boston. Our teachers were pretty much cast from the same mold: late middle-aged or elderly little men and women who had immigrated to America from Russia or Poland many years before. They taught us Hebrew—reading and writing, the Pentateuch, a few scraps of Talmud, a lot of Jewish history, the fine points of ritual and observance of the commandments, as well as a fervent, almost militant Zionism.

Wise-assed little shmuck that I was, I used to find these old characters very comical, very quaint. Only now, much less wise but far better read, do I realize what these little men and women had gone through back in turn-of-the-century Eastern Europe; the violence and turmoil that had scorched them in their childhoods, and the social and political movements that had shaped them in their youth.

In my second year at this school, 1961–1962, my teacher was one Mr. Weissbord. His first name, as I recall, was Morris, but I suspect this was merely what some long dead immigration officer at Ellis Island had done to the name "Moishe." At the time that I had this character to contend with—five days a week, an hour and a half each day—he was probably in his mid- or late 70's. Of course, to our class full of nine and ten-year-olds he seemed *old*, almost impossibly old, old beyond imagining. We often referred to him as *zaydeh*—grandfather, but only behind his back and well out of earshot. You see, Mr. Weissbord was one tough old bird.

Mr. Weissbord was heavy set, probably around five feet six inches, bald headed with a rim of white hair around the sides and back, and red faced with thick course features. His demeanor was what one would perhaps describe as 'severe.' When more or less relaxed, he appeared not only to glower, but indeed to seethe with a barely managed rage of unfathomable depth and texture. When angry, well…you can imagine: a sort of fiery red Mt. Pinatubo sitting on heavy, thick-set shoulders, exploding molten fury with a Russian Yiddish accent. And, there was the…well, *smell*—a *wonderful* smell, a combination of several smells actually, blending into one distinctive scent: sweat, old suit coat, more sweat, Sen-Sen breath mints, and the unfiltered Pall Mall cigarettes that he chain-smoked when he wasn't teaching class. For some reason, I have a vision of him sitting at home, in his apartment on Calendar Street, drinking tea from a samovar out of a glass, with the inevitable cube of sugar in his teeth. The truth is, I never saw him do this, and for all I know he probably stopped drinking tea that way when he said goodbye to Russia some sixty years before. But be that as it may, there's something about that image that would have fit Mr. Weissbord's persona, hand in glove.

As I sit here, some forty years later, trying to conjure up the details of his appearance and the overall aura of his personality, he comes back to me as a kind of cross between Nikita Krushchev and Menachem Begin. My childhood in Dorchester and Mattapan was lavishly resplendent with old Jews of this sort. Sad to say, they don't seem to make them like that any more.

As I mentioned a moment ago, I liked Hebrew School. I liked the history lessons, the songs we were taught, the religious instruction, the Jewishness. I liked learning how to read and write Hebrew—almost like some sort of secret code to my imaginative nine-year-old mind. I liked the books, the maps and pictures of Israel on almost every available piece of wall. Not to mention the writing paper and blank notebooks specially lined for Hebrew letters and vowel marks. I liked the rickety little wooden chairs and tables, with some forty years of carved initials and graffiti. I liked the whole sight, sound, and smell of the place. But most of all, I guess, I liked Mr. Weissbord.

Let's face it, the guy had it all: age, knowledge, and wisdom; an encyclopedic command of Jewish history and heritage; an immigrant background, a thick, borschty Russian accent, and a colorful portfolio of old world characteristics and mannerisms; an intimidating coarseness, a sullen glower, and pyrotechnic explosions of anger—rage as art-form. For the rising young comedian and impressionist that I fancied myself at age nine, Mr. Weissbord was—may God forgive me—great material. Hours and hours of hilarious *shtik*.

To put it simply, I used to "do" Morris Weissbord. You know, the same way John Byner used to "do" Ed Sullivan, the way David Frye "did" Richard Nixon, the way Rich Little "does" almost everyone else. *I* "did" Mr. Weissbord, and I had him down cold. All the gestures, the facial expressions, the temperamental histrionics, and of course the voice, that magnificent *Russhischer* accent, and all of his stock lines and phrases (one of my personal favorites: "You *momzer*!. I pity on you!" I used that line to 'cue my ear,' so to speak). I could even cough and spit like him. **NOW APPEARING…LIMITED ENGAGEMENT…GOOD SEATS STILL AVAILABLE…CARL HOFFMAN *IS* MORRIS WEISSBORD!!!**

I did my Morris Weissbord impressions all over the place, in a variety of venues, wherever I could find an appreciative audience. I played the backyard of the Hebrew school before class, the street out in front of the Hebrew school after class; but most of all, I performed my impressions from my seat, *in* class, while Mr. Weissbord was standing at the front of the room, teaching. The kids in adjacent seats, rubber-necks in nearby rows, anyone and everyone close enough to hear me thought I was absolutely "boffo" and cherished my performances with a reverence comparable only to that accorded by French audiences to Jerry Lewis. I was wild. I was hot. I was *out there*.

As it turned out, my wildest, hottest, and 'out-thereiest' performance occurred in class during one of Mr. Weissbord's more savage displays of ill humor. He was standing in his usual spot, near the blackboard and under a somewhat yellowed portrait of David Ben-Gurion, and screaming at the top of his lungs. The object of his wrath was one "Yehuda" Weinberg (An odd and endearing feature of our Hebrew school was that we almost never knew each other's actual, legal, American first names. We only knew the Hebrew ones that were used in class. Mine was "Zvi"). Weinberg used to sit toward the back of the room, near a corner, his *yarmulke* perpetually askew, and his mind somewhat unhinged. To tell you the truth, I always harbored a mild professional resentment of this kid; he was something of a competing act. *His* entertainment specialties included weird noises, wry comments, loud guffaws, and the ability to toss his pencil up at the ceiling in such a way as to get the point stuck in the acoustical paneling. Show-off.

Damned if I can remember exactly what "Yehuda" Weinberg had done on this occasion, what awful violation of classroom etiquette he had committed, or which of the 613 Talmudic Commandments he had seen fit to flout. Whatever it was, he had Mr. Weissbord almost puking mad and holding on to sanity by a very thin thread. Nostrils flaring, veins bulging, the face darkening to an ominous crimson. Fists clenched, arms raised and jerking violently. The voice raised to a volume we could almost touch and feel, the resonation vibrating through our bodies from our sinuses down to our testicles. The voice rattling the windows and pounding the walls the way typhoon waves pound up on a storm-torn, windswept beach. The voice thrilling, terrifying, and electrifying; we could almost swear that Ben-Gurion's hair was standing up a little more wildly in his portrait than usual. I sat and watched almost trembling with excitement, my creative impulses awakened, my artistic instincts aroused. This moment was made for *me*.

Not that I could have resisted the insistent muse even if I had tried. At almost the instant that Mr. Weissbord had begun to erupt, faces were already turning toward me, hopefully, expectantly. A command performance, as it were, by popular demand. My eyes darted round quickly, taking in my rapidly growing audience—sort of "counting up the house." I glanced up at Mr. Weissbord, letting my fans' anticipation mount, and—of far more importance—satisfying myself that the old man was much too engrossed in his verbal annihilation of "Yehuda" Weinberg to notice the little sideshow *I* was about to put on. Keeping one eye on Mr. Weissbord and the other on my audience, I went into my act.

Seems I've read somewhere that there is a sublime, ineffable moment in which a great actor begins to lose himself in a performance—a magic, almost orgiastic moment in which, for the actor, time stands still and the audience, the physical surroundings, indeed reality itself all but cease to exist. And during this moment, the actor truly looses his identity, his name and his past, as he fuses with the character he is playing and enters his world. Ladies and gentlemen, *I* have known such a moment. *I* have been blessed—if only once—with the heady, indescribable experience of delivering just such a performance. For one or two fleeting minutes, from the humble "stage" of my Hebrew school seat, I *became* Morris Weissbord.

I began, as always, with my stock opening, "You *momzer*, I pity on you!", and proceeded to match Weissbord word for word, gesture for gesture, as he continued to come close to having a brain aneurysm screaming at the Weinberg kid. And if the hysterical snickering of my nearby classmates was any indication, I was "doing" Morris Weissbord better than he had ever "done" himself. But from there I took off, abandoning mere imitation to explore the less trodden paths of improvisation, of uninhibited creativity, and of whimsy. Totally, almost irretrievably absorbed in my art, I was beyond noticing that the laughter had subsided and that the classroom had gone as quiet as the sound of one hand clapping, or in this case, the sound of one hand Mr. Weissbord's—*clenching*, into a tight, meaty fist.

I came to my senses and realized that something was hideously wrong. Mr. Weissbord had apparently pulled himself back from the brink of cardiac arrest by noticing, out of the corner of his eye, an unexpected flurry of activity going on in my sector of the classroom. This old guy had been in the teaching game for years—God only knew how many, and it took him only a split nanosecond to identify the source of this fresh disturbance. Yehuda Weinberg now completely forgotten, Mr. Weissbord stood staring at me as though he'd never seen me—or *anything* quite so repulsive—before.

Mr. Weissbord had caught my act, or the last few seconds of it, and was evidently not amused. You could have used his head for a nightlight the way it seemed to redden and glow. The atmosphere in the room crackled with a strange electricity. The air was pregnant and heavy with impending thunder. My classmates held their breath and thrilled to the tension. I sat there in my seat, looking fearfully up at Mr. Weissbord, fascinated by the throbbing of the veins in his forehead.

When the storm finally broke, it was deafening. Mr. Weissbord started screaming for all he was worth—screaming at me, screaming at the world, and screaming perhaps at the long bitter road that had led him from Odessa to a life teaching Hebrew to incorrigible little savages in Boston. After a minute or so of this, he calmed down a bit, caught his breath and yelled at me, "Alright you *momzer*, you *oysvorf*, I pity on you if there's anything in this week's lessons you wouldn't know. I *pity* on you!"

Then the fun began. Mr. Weissbord began putting me though a kind of spot quiz—more like an inquisition actually—in front of the rest of the class, who were visibly loving every high-drama minute of this and hoping I'd go down in flames. Mr. Weissbord's questions, in Hebrew grammar, reading, Bible, history—whatever the hell he could find quick and grab—came at me like machine gun fire. But so did my answers. All correct.

You see, as I believe I've mentioned, I *liked* Hebrew school. And when I wasn't busy clowning, I was actually paying some attention. So, while the old man was really on his toes at that moment, so was I. Angry question, correct answer. Angry question, correct answer. Question, answer, question, answer…A few of my classmates were actually jerking their heads back and forth as though they were watching a tennis match.

A couple of minutes and God knows how many questions later, Mr. Weissbord got tired. Or maybe he just ran out of things to test me on. Whatever it was, what happened next was extraordinary. Mr. Weissbord stopped shouting, unclenched his fists, and let his arms drop to his sides. He let out a long breath, bobbed his head up and down ever so slightly, and regarded me through shrewd, narrowed eyes. He stood looking at me like this for a while longer, saying nothing, just sort of nodding his head up and down, ever so slightly. And then the weirdest thing started happening to his face: The mouth closed, the lips sort of pursed and tightened, and the whole apparatus began curving upwards, almost imperceptibly, into something resembling a smile. It was a small smile but, by God, a smile just the same.

Was it a smile of admiration, or a sad smile—anticipating the kind of future that awaits most class clowns and incorrigible wise guys? From time to time I remember that smile, and I wonder.

A Poem

1958

Old ladies now, young women then, wrapped in one-piece plastic bathing suits,

    baking themselves an even brown, back to front.

Lazily draped out on plastic plaid-colored beach chairs that seemed

    rooted like the crabgrass, buttercups and dandelions

    to the fragrant ground of our postage stamp-sized backyard.

A slow moving world, molded in plastics, painted in pale pastels.

The young women chat, the young women stretch and yawn.

A bottle of Coppertone, sparkling silkily in the sun, makes its languid transit

    from beach chair to beach chair, while

A song called "volare" wafts softly from a tiny, tinny transistor radio

    and drifts casually away in the heavy summer air.

'Mmmm, wonder where the kids are.'

Kids everywhere, an unending vista of

    sandy-brown crew cuts, flat tops, and ponytails,

    short-shorts, striped jerseys, and baggy dungarees,

    bubble gum, cap guns, baseball cards and hula hoops.

Freckled faces flashing lips turned pastel pink and purple from
    popsicles, icicles, creamsicles and fizzies.

Running, bicycling, bounding and banging into open arms of loving
    aunts and uncles and grandmas and grandpas redolent
    of my sin perfume, of mennen aftershave,
    of dentyne gum, of phillies cigars, and decked out
    in pink slacks and beige bermuda shorts,
    plastic blue haircurlers covered in pink rayon kerchiefs,
    car coats, chinos and cream-colored loafers,
    pale blue butterfly sunglass frames sparkling with sequins
    in the rich golden sunlight of late afternoon.

Relatives all around, as thick as crabgrass.

Too many, too noisy, too desperately affectionate, as if knowing somehow
    that days pass, time flies, and memories must be made for when
    golden days evaporate, when
    kids grow up and relatives live
    only in faded plastic photo albums held together
    with dried-out yellow strips of cellophane tape.

0-595-29064-7

Made in the USA
Columbia, SC
27 November 2022